COASTAL CAPER

COASTAL ADVENTURE SERIES VOLUME 6

DON RICH

Library of Congress PCN Data

Rich, Don

Coastal Caper/Don Rich

(A Mallard Cove Novel)

Florida Refugee Press LLC

Edit/Proofreading by Tim Slauter

Cover Photo by Don Rich

This is a work of fiction. Names, characters, and incidents are either the product of the author's imagination or are used fictitiously. Any resemblance to actual persons, living or dead, businesses, companies, events, or locales is purely coincidental. However, the overall familiarity with boats and water found in this book comes from the author having spent years on, under, and beside them.

Published by FLORIDA REFUGEE PRESS LLC, 2020

Crozet, VA

Copyright © 2020 by Florida Refugee Press LLC

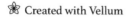 Created with Vellum

To Ed Robinson, author of the three Breeze series, who was taken from us far too soon. I've admired Ed's writing for several years, and chased his books' rankings (with varied success) while he was still with us and producing new volumes. He and I were both original members of TropicalAuthors.com.
Ed left behind a big "back list" of book for us all to enjoy, and that should help to support his family for years to come. If you haven't read him yet, give one of his books a try, you'll be glad you did.

December 12, 2020
Crozet, Virginia

PROLOGUE

I woke up in the master stateroom as normal. But sunlight was already streaming in through a porthole, and the other side of the bed was empty. Neither of these two things were normal, especially on a weekday. I showered, then as I got dressed I realized my wallet wasn't in yesterday's trousers, and my car keys were in the wrong pocket. I searched my dressing room and the stateroom, but the wallet was nowhere to be found. There's no worse feeling with which to start the day than a lost wallet, unless you also have a hangover headache. Which I had. At least I think it's a hangover, I'm not really sure. But as far as my wallet goes, fortunately, we keep a record of everything that's in it in a file at the office. I should be able to get new credit cards sent overnight, and everything else replaced within a week.

I hurried upstairs to grab some carbs to help ease the pounding in my head, plus some caffeine so I can live through the rest of the morning. Dawn was already at the table, finishing up her breakfast.

"Good morning, sunshine, you were sure hooting with the owls last night. You still weren't home when I went to sleep around eleven." she ribbed me. "Have to take a ride-share?"

"Huh?"

"I noticed your Cherokee wasn't here when I walked Bimini this morning."

Bimini is my golden retriever who was now lying next to Dawn's chair, busily gnawing on a huge cow bone.

"I must've, or a cab, I don't remember. But I've never blacked out before, and I guess that's what this is."

Dawn looked concerned. "Blacked out? What's the last thing you remember?"

"Having dinner with Larry Markham at the *Shack*. Then, nothing."

"This isn't like you at all."

"No, it's not. I had a drink before dinner, but I knew I had to drive back, so I was taking it easy especially since it was a Chuck's Martini. I lost my wallet somewhere along the line, too."

Now she was visibly worried. "Do you think you were attacked and robbed?"

"I don't think so, there was only like twenty dollars in cash in it. I don't have a lump on my head, if that's what you mean. And nobody gets robbed in Cape Charles. Though my pistol was locked in my glovebox. I've still got my keys, so my truck should still be there, hopefully with my pistol still in it."

"Could somebody have roofied you? Dropped something in your drink, then robbed you on the way out?"

"Maybe, I don't know. But wouldn't they have stolen my truck as well as my wallet? All they got was that twenty and my credit cards." It was all fuzzy.

She said, "Give me your phone." She looked at something then said, "You took a ride-share from the town docks at ten to midnight. And you left a hundred dollar tip?"

"What the hell was I doing down there at almost midnight? And I wouldn't have tipped the driver a hundred bucks for a twenty-minute ride!"

"Unless your memory comes back, it sounds like we're not going to find out why you were there so late."

Dawn could see how upsetting this was to me; it wasn't my usual behavior. I only went there to have dinner with Markham because he wanted to bring me up to date on a couple of things. I'll be darned if I can remember what those were right now.

"Casey, have some breakfast and let's get to the office so we can cancel your cards. And don't forget that we have a board meeting this morning."

I mumbled, "More like 'try to remember that we have a board meeting,' and I barely do."

Later that morning, two Northampton sheriff's cars pulled up in front of the offices of McAlister and Shaw. Three deputies filed in through the glass front door. Connie Albury, the receptionist, looked up from her desk and addressed them.

"Can I help you gentlemen?"

The first deputy through the door said, "Where is Casey Shaw?"

"Mister Shaw is in a meeting. Would you like to make an appointment?"

Spotting a long hallway off to the left of the reception area, the deputy said, "No." He and his two companions made their way toward it.

"You can't go back there, he's in the middle of a meeting!"

"Stay here," the last deputy said, holding up his palm as he passed her.

Connie picked up her phone and dialed the conference room intercom.

"Casey? Three deputies are on their way back to see you."

I looked up just as the first deputy opened the door. "What's this about?" The other five people seated around the conference table looked equally as confused and curious as I was.

"Are you Casey Shaw?"

"Yes?"

The deputy put one hand on his pistol grip as he moved toward me, the other deputies now filing in behind him. "Stand up, sir, and put your hands behind your back." As I cautiously stood, the first deputy moved around behind me and pulled my hands together roughly, then handcuffed me.

"Casey Shaw, you are under arrest for the murder of Mayor Robert Shalloway of Cape Charles. You have the right to remain silent, anything you say can and will be used against you..."

As I was being shoved through the doorway, Eric Clarke asked the last deputy, "Where are you taking him?"

"To the Sheriff's Office in Northampton county."

Eric hit a number programmed into his phone. "Greg? Who do you know that's the best criminal defense lawyer in Virginia? Howard Falcon? Okay, we need him right now for Casey. Yeah, Shaw. Un huh. They said for murder."

1

DEVELOPMENT RULES

L ynnhaven, VA, a week and a half prior...

I WATCHED AS THE LARGE, track-footed excavators dug scoop after scoop of soil out of what will soon become our marina basin here at Lynnhaven, Virginia. Dump truck load after dump truck load of material was being hauled up and out via an earthen ramp, to be spread around the rest of the project's acreage. This area is subject to flooding during some of the larger storms that hit the mid-Atlantic. Keeping the material on-site and using it to raise our property will make the stores, apartments, condos, hotel, and restaurant spaces here that much more desirable.

The outline of the marina basin has become apparent as huge mechanical vibrating arms have been driving thick, interlocking corrugated "sheet piles" into the ground, forming the bulkheads. These will be capped with concrete and backfilled with more of the material that we're removing from the basin.

By the way, my name is Casey Shaw. I'm approaching my middle-forties, but I've been a real estate investor in my native Florida for over twenty-five years. Yeah, I started young. Renovating and holding properties is what I've primarily done up until I moved up here to Virginia, two years ago.

I left because I had tired of seeing the great old buildings in my native West Palm Beach erased, only to be replaced by tall glass and concrete "human filing cabinets." These tacky structures seem to fill as fast as they went up, attracting northern transplants who have no regard for the way things were before they arrived, and no desire to learn about it.

In the first forty years of my life, I watched as Palm Beach County added over a million people, and the Southern culture that had been such a large part of our lives swiftly faded into the past. Our laid-back lifestyle surrendered to the hustle and bustle that is the accepted culture of the northeast, and crime and gang violence became more rampant. I knew it was time to leave before I began losing my own identity as well. You can only live in a swamp for so long before the muck stops washing off.

I've got a confession to make; I'm somewhat complicit in the changes that created that swamp. Though I never was the one who tore down and erased those last vestiges of our culture, I sold a lot of it to the people who did. I learned a long time ago to buy in the path of progress, renovate and restore what is there so you can get the highest rents and income possible while you hold the properties and wait for them to appreciate.

I moved up to the Eastern Shore of Virginia with that same idea in mind. I bought an old inn and marina, and turned it into a high-end property called the *Chesapeake Bayside Resort*. Then I bought another marina and renovated it as well, turning it into *The Bluffs Marina & Restaurant*. Along the way, I brought in some very talented people as partners. Together we recently bought the four hundred acres next to *Bayside* where we're creating an exclusive club and spa with a private marina and a hundred-twenty mini-estates. While this crossed over the line and I became a developer by doing that, I still stuck to my principles. I didn't tear down or erase any buildings, and I've made sure our group has adopted that principle as our own now, too. The project here in Lynnhaven is being built on the last large vacant waterfront parcel left in the area.

While this is a huge project, it won't feel crowded when it's finished. We want people to be drawn to our properties to relax, and they can't do that if they feel jammed into a tightly crowded area. Our properties are fun and laid back, even our *Bayside Club and Spa*. While it's extremely high end, it's also mostly what we call "Chesapeake Casual" instead of ultra-dressy. Many of our clientele are from Washington, DC, and they get enough of that there. We laid out our *Bayside Estates* as lower density too, with plenty of greenspace between each homesite. In fact, we set aside almost two-thirds of the initial acreage in a conservation easement leaving it mostly natural except for miles of grass trails for riding bicycles and horses or just walking. Relaxation is one of the hallmarks of the brand we're building. "Chesapeake Casual" is the way I like to live my life; jeans, khakis, and vented fishing shirts are my favorite attire in the warmer months.

My looks as well as my dress are in contrast to the person next to me this morning; I'm six-feet tall, and my hair is kind of a longish sandy mop. Getting my hair cut has never been high on my list of things to do on any day. But standing next to me is a young woman who stands out for several reasons. First, she's very young and beautiful, with long black hair that never seems to have a strand out of place. She has a great figure that turns heads whenever she wants it to or is camouflaged when she doesn't. Like today on this job-site where she's dressed in loose-fitting pants and a long sleeve oxford. But while my jeans and shirt are a bit rumpled, her clothes still have the knife-edge creases left by an iron and plenty of spray starch. She's also six inches shorter than me height-wise, though she's quickly becoming equal in stature to me within our real estate business. A business where she's proven herself to be as sharp as the creases in her clothes. It's the reason she's the head of M&S Partners, our private company that acquires, designs, develops, and manages marina properties around the Chesapeake and mid-Atlantic coasts.

Pretty darn impressive for someone who is barely over a quarter-century old.

Before you get the wrong idea, my companion today isn't also my girlfriend, but one of my partners in a couple of real estate ventures including the one we're standing in the middle of. Her name is Kari Albury. Er, I mean, Kari Denton. She married a friend of mine a few weeks back, Marlin Denton. Kari came to our company as a receptionist, but we quickly recognized that she had tremendous and wasted potential. Kari has that rare ability to look at a property and not only see it for what it is, but for what it can be. That's a gift that both she and I share.

Kari was in charge of the redesign of our *Mallard Cove Marina* property; she added restaurants, bars, a hotel, and a boat dry storage barn. *Mallard Cove* has now become the "happening" place to go on the Eastern Shore of Virginia, better known as ESVA, especially on the weekends in the summer. It's because of Kari's ability to unlock hidden value in properties that she also designed and is overseeing this current project, her largest assignment to date.

And now she has me interested in yet another property that she recently discovered on ESVA up in Cape Charles. We're headed there after we finish up here this morning. About the only thing that Cape Charles has in common with Lynnhaven is that it's on the water. Lynnhaven is on the north side of Virginia Beach, and just east of Norfolk. The area is pretty congested, and you have to time your car trips around here to avoid rush hour backups and snarls.

Cape Charles, on the other hand, is a small and quiet beach town of five hundred houses. Instead of being surrounded by other towns, it's in the middle of farms and woods near the end of the peninsula. But it's a town that's undergoing big changes. Twenty years ago you could have had your pick of vacant buildings downtown, literally for pennies on today's dollars. But now they've all been bought and renovated. They're either filled or filling up with quaint shops and unique restaurants. There are bakeries, a microbrewery, numerous gift shops, a couple of boutique hotels, and real estate offices. Yes, I mean plural on real estate offices. That's the real tipoff that things are far from done around there. If the town wasn't open for expansion, and the outlying area not ripe for development, there's no way that more than one real estate office could survive off of only five-hundred houses.

Kari stumbled across the biggest plum there is, the old railroad yards that had been the southern terminus of the old ESVA railroad. Before the creation of the seventeen-mile-long Chesapeake Bay Bridge-Tunnel that opened back in the nineteen-sixties, the railroad was an important part of the supply line for ESVA. But instead of having to make the trip all the way down the peninsula, huge barges were loaded with rail cars in Norfolk, then tugboats towed them the twenty-six miles to the wharf here where they were loaded and unloaded. In fact, it was the railroad company that built the town of Cape Charles, back in the late eighteen-hundreds.

But the opening of the CBBT sounded the death knell for the eventual end of the need for rail traffic between Norfolk and Cape Charles. Cargo coming through the town, which at one point reached two and a half million tons per year, now shipped cheaper and easier via semi-trucks. And the railroad decided to cut its losses, selling the property to the town.

But here's where it gets tricky. Kari discovered the town intends to get it developed to increase their tax base. After all, you can garner only so much tax revenue from a railroad siding. Adding condos, commercial space, and a marina there will mean a huge increase in real estate taxes and jobs. So the property will now be generating sales tax income as well, not to mention the hundreds of new customers for the town's utility company.

The town stands to now make hundreds of thousands of dollars annually from this hundred-acre property, where before it was only bringing in a tiny percentage of that. Sounds like a no-brainer, right? Build the heck out of the parcel, squeezing in every square inch of building as possible. But doing that would be a huge mistake in both Kari's and my opinions. They need to be very careful with what they allow to be built; whoever develops it needs to be mindful and considerate of what already surrounds it. A large portion of that parcel borders the small main street, and whatever goes in there needs to fit in. By that I mean not just with the existing architecture, but with the price points of the existing businesses. The people who own those buildings and businesses have not just money invested in them but bits of their lives. Hopes, dreams, personal sacrifices, these are all some of the currency that's gone into building these small businesses as the owners rebuilt and reshaped the town's future. They're all part of what needs to be carefully protected. Done properly, the rail yard project will only add to the value of these businesses and properties. But if it's done wrong, they could quickly lose what they've worked so hard to build. And there are a bunch of developers who wouldn't care if they got it wrong, so long as the check cashed before they got the heck out of town.

My past down in Florida gives me a unique perspective as to what can go wrong with redevelopment; most people can't understand that unless you've lived through it. You mention West Palm Beach and instantly they get this vision of glitz, glamor, and wealth. Yet a recent poll showed a surprisingly high number of the county residents would move out of there if they could afford to. Many have had enough of the hurricanes, crime, and congestion, or a combination of the three. I know a lot of natives like myself that have already left.

Instead of capitalizing on the laid-back culture that existed, the developers bulldozed it all. Granted, in Florida's case, the thing most people were looking for was a warm winter with no snow to shovel. Had they just taken the time to look at what was already there and built on that base, it would be a much better place than it is. Many new transplants see it as paradise but if they'd only seen it back when I was a kid, they'd feel differently about it now.

My views on the subject are a large part of why Kari and I work together so well. She's an ESVA native, what they refer to as a "born here." I, on the other hand, am a "come here," something that will never change. We had a similar system down in Florida when I was a kid, before all of us natives became so outnumbered. It used to mean something to be a native back then, and up here it still does. Even though it means I'll always be an outsider, I hope they never lose this here, because I understand all too well what happens when you do.

Kari is an Albury, a multi-generational native of one of the largest and oldest families on ESVA. As a "born here" she has access to a huge network of people that I don't. Because of her involvement, a few of her cousins now work in our organization. Yet another cousin is the sheriff of Accomack county where *Bayside* is located. While Kari's an equity partner in our projects, she's also the last person who would want to profit at the expense of the culture and identity of ESVA. She and I have had long conversations about this subject, and we share the same concerns. Her views have also earned her a level of trust among the residents where we operate on ESVA, and our company has benefitted through this as well. I'm hoping that this will now extend to Cape Charles, too. We're about to find out if it will.

2

BACK ROOM DEAL

I t's been a while since I've been to Cape Charles, and I had forgotten how much I like the little town. I was driving, but as we approached, instead of going directly to the rail yard Kari directed me to turn north then west, skirting the edge of the historic residential section of town.

"See how they walled it off, Casey? Trees, fence, and a moat."

Kari was talking about a large, partially built-out development on the north side of town. At the time it was planned, the residential part of town hadn't become as attractive to real estate investors as it is now. Many of these renovated houses have since become weekly summer rentals, and the competition for vacationers' business is fierce. Almost all the properties are booked solid through the season and around the end of year holidays. But I could see exactly what she meant about the development. Meaning, I could only see glimpses of it through the trees and across the lake that lined the right side of the road. It looked like a completely separate town with similar tall and brightly colored houses all packed closely together, so I could see why it appears to be stalled. They all looked the same, almost "cookie-cutter" style.

Kari continued, "The rail yard is right downtown, so whatever we would do needs to embrace the architectural feel and look of what's right across the street. These guys should have done that. They really blew it by disregarding the historic look and feel of the town, which is what people want now. We're less than two hours from Richmond, and half an hour from Norfolk, Hampton, and Virginia Beach. But unlike the hustle and bustle of VA Beach, this is such a relaxed little beach town, perfect for weekend places. Whatever we do needs to fit in."

We reached the end of Washington Avenue and followed the left-hand curve as it became Bay Avenue. A narrow sand and scrub median runs down the middle of the street. For its six-block length this two-lane street's parking area is lined down both sides with cars and golf carts. The carts are a favorite mode of transportation in town where the speed limit is twenty-five. Just beyond the sidewalk on the beach side is a head-high sand dune covered with beach grasses, creating a nice privacy screen from the road for the beachgoers. We could see only occasional glimpses of the Chesapeake down the half-dozen walking paths that cut through the dune.

Halfway down the road on the right and sticking partly out into our lane was a large octagonal bandstand stage/pavilion with an elevated floor and a wooden roof. Then at the end of Bay Avenue, the road turned back east and became Mason Avenue, the main drag through downtown. On the right at the curve was a long wooden fishing pier at the mouth of the harbor. Next to that was the large Cape Charles' iconic "LOVE" sculpture, comprised of crab traps, kayak hulls, a tractor tire, and oyster shells. Extremely popular, there is hardly a daylight hour that goes by without someone taking a selfie in front of it, or kids climbing on it. Google "Cape Charles, VA" and it's one of the first things that comes up in the image results.

So, if you were to design the perfect little boutique beach and the town to go along with it, Cape Charles would fill the bill. There's no boardwalk, and in this town that's a very good thing. If you want tee shirts and french fry shops, you need to go to Ocean City, Maryland, or Rehoboth Beach, Delaware. This isn't nearly as crowded on its worst day, which makes it that much better. There aren't any parasail boats, sailing head-boats, or raucous bars. You can find all that fifteen minutes away at *Mallard Cove*. This was somewhere in between that and our *Bayside* property. More of a laid back clientele than *Mallard Cove*, but not nearly as expensive as *Bayside*. A niche that our organization had yet to fill on ESVA. I liked what I saw.

I parked my vintage Jeep Cherokee and we walked back to the pier, stopping just beyond the base of the dune. Looking down the curved beach, in the distance I could see the top floors of a few of the taller multi-story houses along Bay Avenue. Several snow fences were spaced along the dune, their ends disappearing back in the sand. Probably put there to help hold it in place until the wild grasses had taken root, stabilizing it.

The beach was about forty-yards-wide from the dune grasses to a weed line that marked the high tide apex. The tide was out now, exposing another sixty or seventy yards of wet sand and small tidal pools beyond, before the edge of the drop off into the Chesapeake where it gets deep very quickly. At flood tide this exposed sandbar becomes a giant wading pool, perfect for kids to play on, and a great place for adults to sit and relax, on the sand or in a semi-submerged beach chair. Like I said, the perfect little boutique beach.

Looking back southeast toward the rail yard and the harbor, I can envision a new marina with stair-stepped buildings beyond. Also, a line of mixed-use buildings of varied styles and materials, with none of the same color or style of brick used more than twice. All designed to look like they had been built separately over time, just like those on the other side of the street. We need to match the quaintness of the main street, keeping the same feel that draws the current clientele. Don't reinvent the wheel, just add another parallel one.

We got back in the Jeep, moving it halfway down the street before parking, then we walked out to the middle of the property. For both Kari and me, it was a little like walking into a vision, imagining much the same thing as we looked around.

Again we got back into the Jeep and drove slowly up Mason Avenue, alongside the multi-block long property. We looked over across the parcel to the town harbor beyond. I suddenly realized that

Kari and I had both been silent ever since we got back into the truck. I said, "I see it. Great find, by the way. Now, let's go see if we can buy it."

Kari directed me down to a side street to the town hall where we found a parking place across the street. As we got out and headed for the office, one of the last people I wanted to see here right now was walking out the front door. Kari saw him at the same time and exclaimed, "Aw, damn! That's Glenn Cetta."

From the look on his face when he spotted Kari, the feeling was mutual. "Birddog" Cetta owned several marinas and other real estate around the Chesapeake. He had come after *Mallard Cove Marina* just as our partners tied up the deal. He then tried to get the seller to break the contract and sell it to him instead. Cetta ended up making one of our partners, Lindsay Davis, angry enough to start heaving fishing weights at him there on the dock, scoring a direct hit on his butt from ten yards away. It was a large egg-shaped lead, and I guarantee he felt that one every time he sat down for the next few days.

Ironically, Lindsay and her boyfriend, Michael "Murph" Murphy, later negotiated a deal for their home, a house barge, through one of Cetta's marina managers, scoring yet again. This time though the hit was to his wallet since he had been so anxious to sell it and they were the only interested party. He didn't know who the buyers were until they arrived to tow it back to *Mallard Cove*. At that point, Cetta threw a lot of curses and threats at them until Kari, who was on the pickup crew, let loose with a few of her own. She also reminded Cetta of how accurate Lindsay was with lead sinkers, at which point "Birddog" decided to retreat.

Our group crossed paths with him again when we bought both the vacant Lynnhaven parcel and the marina next door. Cetta had owned the marina for years, hoping to add the adjacent property to it and build something like we were doing. After finally giving up on the idea, he finally sold it to someone who would then toss in with us and become a member of our investment group for that property. We had realized Cetta's unfulfilled dream of combining the two parcels. We were able to accomplish this because the vacant property's owner had taken such a severe dislike to Cetta that he had refused to sell, at any price. I heard that when Cetta found out we had bought both properties, he went ballistic. Again. And there was only one reason for him to be coming out of that door right now; we were after the same property. Again. He switched from staring at Kari over to me, his jaw first dropping before eventually clenching in anger. He knew why we were both here.

"You! But you aren't even on the list! Not that it matters, since Bob wants me to be the one to develop that property; you're just wasting your time."

We walked toward him as he reached the door of his Range Rover. I asked him, "What list? Who is Bob?"

He sneered as he climbed into the driver's seat. "Since you're here, you'll find out, smart guy. You'll also see that you're wasting your time, this deal's already done."

Cetta slammed the door and quickly drove off, leaving Kari and I standing on the sidewalk. She looked amused and said, "Well, we won't find any answers out here. Let's see if we can find out who this 'Bob' is, and what he has to do with that property."

We entered the office and asked the receptionist who we should see to talk about the railroad yard property. She made a call, and told us that the mayor would be with us in a few minutes, and motioned us over to a pair of old, very uncomfortable wooden chairs.

Ten minutes later a short, pudgy, middle-aged man approached. He had a bad toupee, and his hair color had come from a bottle, right down to his mustache. "I'm Mayor Robert Shalloway, how can I help you two?" His tone dripped with self-importance and implied that being helpful was not his strong suit. Having just met the man, I already didn't like him for years. Fortunately, Kari spoke for us.

"We're from M&S Partners, and we're interested in purchasing the old railroad parcel."

Shalloway looked up and down Kari the same way a wolf looks at a sheep. He was one creepy bastard. "Yes, well, the town has already identified a very qualified list of developers that we are in talks with over that parcel, and M&S isn't one of them."

"Really. And why is that Mister Shalloway?"

"*Mayor* Shalloway. And that would be because we don't like your building style, and feel that you lack the necessary capital to complete a project of this size."

Now I was pissed. "Excuse me, but just how would you know how much capital we may or may not have access to? And just what do you think our 'building style' is, since we evaluate each project and adapt the style to fit in with the surroundings."

He was in a hurry to shut us down. "It doesn't matter since you aren't on the list for consideration at tonight's town council meeting. Now if you'll excuse me, I have a very busy morning." Behind him, I saw the receptionist roll her eyes. Apparently, he wasn't very popular in the office.

Kari asked, "Well, how do we go about getting on that list?"

He smirked, "I personally vetted and assembled the list for the council's consideration, and everyone that is on it has my personal approval. I can assure you that you won't be getting on it."

I said, "I'd like to see the list."

He bristled. "It's none of your business!"

"Actually, it is. I have a contract on another property here in Cape Charles, which means I have a vested interest in what happens here. According to the 'government in the sunshine' laws, documents such as your list are all in the public domain. I'd like to see that list now, or if you want to give me the name of the town's lawyer I'll have my lawyer call and explain exactly why you need to hand it over." I could see Shalloway's neck then cheeks starting to get red. He stomped over to a clerk, then returned with a single sheet agenda for tonight's meeting, including a list of speakers with development proposals. He silently thrust it at me.

Kari and I looked over the list then I said, "I know everyone on this list. Talk about not having access to the necessary capital! The only one who could handle a project of this size is Cetta. I thought you said you vetted all that were on it."

"I did! And everyone on that list has adequate resources." This time, he didn't sound quite as self-assured as he had been a minute before.

I said, "Really? Then I guess you missed the fact that Peterson Brothers filed for bankruptcy last Friday. You know, the company that is second from the top of the list? So, I wouldn't hold my breath, expecting them to show up tonight."

Kari looked curiously at Shalloway. "Is your wife's name Cheryl?"

Shalloway recoiled, looking very nervous. He mumbled a reply that I couldn't make out.

"Now I know where I've seen you before, it was in the ESVA Herald. You and your wife hosted a charity fundraiser at your home. I remembered her name was Cheryl. Cheryl Cetta-Shalloway. I'm guessing that 'Birddog' is a family member. A brother perhaps," Kari asked.

The red in Shalloway's face was quickly receding, and he was becoming very pale. "Glenn is a very qualified candidate, and being related to my wife shouldn't disqualify him. That wouldn't be fair to him, or the town."

I said, "And our lack of being related to her or you shouldn't disqualify us either. You need to put us on that list, and I mean like right now."

He regained a bit of composure before saying, "It's not like it's gonna do you any good. They're all coming tonight bringing their proposals and renderings. You can't show up with nothing in hand and expect to be taken seriously."

Kari said, "Let us worry about that part. Just put us on the list, or we'll take out a full-page ad in the next Herald, explaining exactly what you're doing here. I bet the Commonwealth Attorney over in Richmond would love to get involved since it's an election year."

"Fine. You can speak last, right after Glenn. You'll be laughed out of the council chamber."

I replied, "Let us worry about that. Now put us on the damn list, and I want a copy of the new one before we leave."

· · ·

BACK IN MY JEEP, I asked Kari, "We can be ready to make a presentation tonight, right? I mean, renderings and all?"

"I've already got a first draft, complete with renderings. I put it all together after I first saw the property. Drop me back at my office, and I'll tighten them up. Don't worry, we'll be ready. And by the way, when did you go to contract on a property here in Cape Charles?"

"Well, I'm thinking about buying one of our condos after they're built. So, it's kind of a verbal contract." I couldn't help but grin, and she returned it.

3
___

SMALL TOWN POLITICS

7 p.m. that evening at the Cape Charles Town Hall

I HATE TOWN MEETINGS. Lots of political fodder and drama for public consumption, but as you've already seen, much goes on in the background and in the back rooms. The first item voted on in the meeting is usually something called a "consent agenda," and tonight it passed unanimously. It's where they hide things that they can later point to and say, "*Well, we voted on it out in the open for everybody to see!*" Yeah, right, as long as you're crafty enough to get your hands on the more detailed version of that agenda than the one they hand out to the audience.

But awarding the future of a huge parcel of land is not something that could be hidden within a consent agenda. Shalloway had done the next best thing by lining up a list of mostly unqualified developer-wannabes who would never make it past any second public vetting, leaving his brother-in-law as the sole surviving candidate. Yes, Cetta was indeed his brother in law; Kari had confirmed that through her network of ESVA contacts.

As it turned out, we weren't the only ones upset about not being invited to the party, another registered Virginia development company had their attorney present at the meeting to object to their exclusion from the selection process. When they questioned why no one from the company was in attendance, the lawyer said the company's management group and the chief counsel from his office were all at a similar meeting up in New Jersey, where they had a large project underway. He explained he had been called in at the last minute to represent his client.

If the company is doing work up in New Jersey, I wondered how they would have even heard about this parcel, much less be interested enough to send an attorney to the meeting. But the lawyer was still allowed to address the council and get his client's position across, and they agreed to hear their proposal at the next meeting in two weeks if they could submit a packet a week before. Sure, the "out-of-towners" get an extra week to prepare, but we have to present tonight. There's nothing like placing your bet after you've already seen everybody else's cards, and nobody has so much as even seen you. The only reason they're getting to present at all is because the town council apparently is afraid of lawyers. A fact I'm filing away for later use if I need it.

It quickly became obvious the first six proposals were being made by contractors who had no prior development experience. Oh sure, they had been *around* developers and worked building houses within different developments, but there's a huge difference between being a homebuilder or a developer. With *Bayside Estates* already selling nicely and the *Lynnhaven* project firmly underway, our team had some good development experience to point to. Kari was a terrific team leader, but Glenn Cetta, well, not so much. His vision for the rail yards was grandiose and modernistic with lots of glass and white marble. His marina plan was geared mostly toward mega-yachts, meaning one-hundred-fifty-feet and longer. Everything about his proposal was ultra-high-end and futuristic, right down to the commercial spaces that would line Mason Avenue. I could see from his expression this was exactly what Shalloway wanted for Cape Charles. Sadly, I couldn't think of anything worse.

While I could easily read Shalloway, the rest of the town council would make great poker players; I had no idea which way they were leaning. But from the murmur of the audience, I knew there were a few folks that were intrigued by Cetta's plan, and that worried me.

Kari and I decided earlier that I'd go first, laying out how we had come up with our vision for the rail yards. I figured that a straight attack on Cetta's concept would turn more of the council against us than it would win over, and we knew we were starting with at least one vote already against us.

I began by telling them about our company, and how our properties are so successful, because we know who our customers are, and who they would continue to be. Then I complimented them on their success in revitalizing Cape Charles, and how we wanted to build on that success by embracing what they've already done; targeting families and active retirees who want to escape to ESVA for the weekend or the week. Then Kari got up and presented her renderings of what we wanted to build, and told of how it would fit in, doubling the size of the downtown and increasing the lure, not just from within the town but from the surrounding areas. She had revenue projections for the new commercial properties as well as a boutique hotel that was included in our plan since the new businesses would help create demand that would outstrip the number of currently available hotel rooms.

Kari continued, sharing her research about how much they could expect in business from each boat that stayed in the new marina, and why it was important to target the more common family-sized cruisers and outboards. She specifically cautioned them about targeting mega-yachts. Kari pointed out that unlike cruise ships, mega-yachts aren't packed with people, though they take up a tremendous amount of marina space. Plus, a marina aiming at mega-yachts can be very off-putting to other boaters. No one wants to have the smallest boat at the dock or feel like they don't belong there.

I saw that our concept was now getting some favorable looks from the other four council members. Shalloway and Cetta both looked like they wanted us dead. But if the town went with us and our design, I knew they'd be avoiding a potential disaster. I saw the other company's lawyer had been taking notes and pictures of Kari's presentation. Yeah, there's nothing like having someone else do your homework for you. That really ticked me off. But I felt that our presentation had been the best, and now we just have to wait and see what the last group comes in with.

"HOW DID IT GO?" My fiancée, Dawn McAlister asked as I walked in. Home is *Lady Dawn*, a one-hundred-ten-foot Hargrave yacht which wis docked at *Bayside Marina*.

"You should have seen the look on Cetta's face when Kari finished up, he was about to blow a circuit. I'm so glad she's on the team."

Dawn kissed me and smiled. Only an inch shy of six-feet, with blue eyes and long red hair, she's stunning. But she's as sharp at business as she is beautiful. When we opened *Bayside* last year, *Chesapeake Bay Today* magazine dubbed us "*ESVA's new power couple.*" I can tell you, it wasn't because of me. "*My better half*" doesn't begin to describe what she is to me.

She said, "I figured you'd be tired, so we've got dinner waiting in the galley."

I laughed, "That's what you get for hooking up with an old guy." I'm only forty-three, but I'm still thirteen years older than her. It's not an issue between us, though her father's not pleased. I get along with him to a point, but I know I'm not his first choice for her. The McAlisters are an old Eastern Shore of Maryland family from up in Easton, and tradition runs deep within them. I think he's happy that we haven't gotten married yet, figuring there's still a chance we won't. He'd be smart not to bet on that.

Eating at the crew table in the galley when it's just the two of us having a late dinner together is one of my favorite things. It's more relaxed, and we can sit closer in the u-shaped booth. Over dinner, I related what happened at the meeting in-depth.

"Casey, that's really strange. A development group from here we've never heard of that's working up in New Jersey? And why send an attorney to the meeting instead of one of their planners?"

"Sending a lawyer makes sense if they wanted to intimidate the town council into allowing them to present their plan after a delay. But I still don't get how they would have heard about it if they're busy working up in New Jersey, when we're not thirty miles away and yet we had to stumble onto it by chance. Unless they plan on investing more around here and are already digging." There was something about this that wasn't sitting well with me. Not all of it was about them seeing our plans two weeks before they present theirs.

Dawn looked thoughtful, "I'll jump on it tomorrow and see what I can find out about them. You think there's more to this, don't you?"

I nodded. "I've got a funny feeling that we need to watch our backs on this one. I don't know what it is about it, but I want to find out all we can. We've blindsided Cetta a few times, and I don't want it to become our turn."

THE NEXT MORNING I got a call from Larry Markham, one of the Cape Charles councilmen, asking if I could meet him for an early lunch at the *Shack* restaurant. This is a great seafood restaurant next to the rail yards overlooking the harbor at the town marina, and we agreed on eleven o'clock. He was standing outside the door with another man as I drove up. The second guy turned out to be Bill Withers, the owner of the *Shack*. Bill led us to a private dining room where we could eat and speak in private. I got the feeling that Bill had a lot of pull in town, and it wasn't long before Larry confirmed that.

"Casey, Bill's a little concerned about the possibility of a competing seafood restaurant going in next door at the rail yards. So far Cetta isn't willing to say whether or not they're planning on putting one in if they get the project."

I said, "By 'they,' I take it you mean Cetta and..." I didn't even get the chance to finish my sentence.

Withers almost yelled, "That sonofabitch Shalloway, that's who!

He's trying to ramrod this thing and put me out of business in the process." Clearly, there was no love lost between the two.

"What about the other groups," I asked?

Markham tilted his head slightly, "There are no other groups. Those guys were all there last night as window dressing for the *Herald*, so it wouldn't be so blatantly obvious that it was Shalloway up to his old tricks again. They're Cetta's contractors; he supplied them with their so-called 'proposals.' Shalloway's been getting away with this kind of crap for years, just on a smaller scale. This is his big play. Then when he's eventually off the council, he'll suddenly end up owning the lion's share of the deal."

I asked, "What do you want from me?"

Withers replied, "A guarantee that you won't put another seafood place in the project to compete with the *Shack*."

I knew better than to ask, *What do I get in return?* It was written on Markham's face; our proposal will have his support. And while this meeting was legal since there was only one council member present because of those "government in the sunshine laws," I'm willing to bet that Withers may have some pull with at least one other council member. But I wanted more info before I started giving things away.

"What about that other group?"

Markham replied, "You mean the one that nobody's ever heard of? Here's the deal Casey, while you're a 'come here,' at least you live here, and you showed up in person. And that young lady you have working for you is impressive as hell, not to mention being a 'born here' from a well-respected family."

"While she does technically work for me, she's also a partner in the group."

He looked surprised, "Even better. I'll make sure the others know that as well."

The others. As in, plural. Probably meaning at least two of the other council members that we'd need to end up with the deal. If all it costs me is an agreement with Withers, I'll be a very happy fellow. I turned to him, "Bill, if we get the deal, I'll own at least one restaurant in the complex, and every restaurant around the water has to have at least some seafood on its menu. But I think we can draw up an agreement stating that we won't allow any restaurant to have more than a quarter of its menu consist of seafood, so long as you still own and operate the *Shack*. We'll make it a stipulation in each lease. Think that would work for you?"

A very relieved Bill Withers smiled and stuck out his hand, which I shook. Markham looked relieved as well. If we hadn't made a deal, it would have put him in the very difficult position of having to vote for Cetta, or voting for our project, even though it would've burned Wither's butt.

After a fantastic seafood lunch that Withers wouldn't let me pay for, I first started to go to my office up at *Bayside,* but instead went to see Kari at her office down at *Mallard Cove.* I wanted to share that we had some crucial support for the project, but I also needed her to whip up a rendering of an addition to the project. It might be worth a little more information.

A CURIOUS BILL WITHERS walked me back into his office when I returned so unexpectedly. After we both sat down I said, "I'm guessing that you get a decent amount of business from people over in downtown that have to walk across the rail yard."

"We do, and probably will up until the point your project gets built. I'm hoping they'll be willing to drive around to get to us."

I grinned, "They won't have to if my design gets chosen." I handed him the newly updated renderings showing a two-story-high breezeway tunnel cutting through the largest building, a four-story complex. The breezeway ended in the parking lot that the *Shack* and the marina share. "This solves a lot of problems for us, adding window frontage along the breezeway for additional retail space in the center of the building. And it'll be wide enough for both pedestrians and golf carts. Of course, it wasn't part of the original concept, so it would need to be approved by the council, and that's a moot point if we don't get the property."

It was his turn to grin. "Last time I checked, you didn't need more than three of the four votes you already have. Though Shalloway is going to be a lifelong enemy of yours. Fortunately, his term as mayor is up this year, so he will be less of an irritation. For all of us."

~

JOEY NEWELL CALLED the Virginia attorney who attended last night's meeting. "So, whadda you find out?"

"I'm emailing you the pictures of the two projects."

Joey's thick New Jersey accent couldn't cover his surprise. "I thought there was gonna be like seven of 'em?"

"I'm not certain exactly what happened, but six of them didn't even appear to be serious, they weren't that well-presented, and judging by the faces on the council, they weren't impressed. The one by Cetta and Associates was very professional, and there was another last-minute addition, M&S Partners. It looked like there was no love lost between those two. Though Cetta wasn't happy about us, either."

Joey stroked his chin thoughtfully. "You mean me. So, the first six were crap, huh? And this M&S bunch was late to the party. Sounds like somebody had themselves a smokescreen until I showed up. Small town politics, I love it. Lets ya know who the real players are, real quick."

"If I had to guess, I'd say that Cetta was in the mayor's camp."

"Guess? At five-hundred an hour, I ain't payin' you to guess. I wanna know who's what to who, you got that," Joey demanded.

"I understand. I'll have more for you by the time you arrive."

Joey said, "You better have everything by the time I get there, I'm not payin' you to sit on your ass! I'm gonna be stayin' at the *Bayside Resort*, they got a helipad there. I'm gonna chopper the Chief over, show him more about who his new partner is, and that I ain't playin' around. So, get your stuff together, I don't want no holes in this plan, you got me?"

"I understand. Everything will be ready when you arrive."

4

MAKING FRIENDS

Dawn did a lot of digging around, trying to find out more about the competition, but there wasn't a lot of information to be had. The lawyer may have slipped when he said that his client was working in New Jersey; the face of everything about this group all read "Virginia." Their new Limited Liability Corporation was registered in Richmond, and their Virginia attorney was listed as the manager and registered agent. Their bank account only had one signer, that Richmond attorney. Whoever is behind that company is sure going to a lot of trouble to avoid being identified. That funny feeling I originally had was growing stronger.

I had a lot to do here at the office this week, but I know a bit about small-town politics. Spending time and showing interest in Cape Charles between now and their next council meeting is very important. Yes, I know Bill Withers said that we have four out of five council votes already, but if that's true I intend to keep it that way. The only "unknown" in all of this is that last group, and the only face they're showing is that high-dollar lawyer. Not something to reassure a small town council about who they're dealing with. I want to make sure the council members see both Kari and me around town, having meals and talking with people. I want to raise the comfort level of all the townspeople with both us and our project.

Without a doubt, it would be a good idea to get Dawn down there with me, too. As tall as she is, and with her long, bright red hair, she's easily spotted and not easily forgotten. And a lot of people there would probably remember her from that *Chesapeake Bay Today* article, too. Between the three of us, we are going to put a "face" on our proposal. The last thing we need is to be thought of as is a soulless corporation, or even worse, a bunch of out of town carpetbaggers. But that's exactly how we want that unknown bunch to be seen. So, the sooner we all start spending some time there, the better.

I walked into Dawn's office, "Hey, can you spare a few hours today? I want us and Kari to start getting better known down at Cape Charles."

"Not a bad idea, Case. I haven't been in most of those shops. I can call Lindsay too, since she and Murph are in this deal, and we can make the rounds and do some shopping at the same time. It'll be good research as well as public relations."

"Just remember, the object of this is to make a profit, not spend it all in those shops before we even break ground," I ribbed her.

"Oh, like you won't be snagging the latest lure or a new cast net in the tackle shop," she retorted.

I said, "Oh, right, there's a tackle shop! I should see if Murph wants to come along, too."

Dawn frowned at the idea, but only briefly. As well as being my best friend, Murph is also Dawn's ex-fiancée. The full story is a long one for another day, but the condensed version is Murph worked for me down in Florida for fifteen years. That's where he met Dawn and hired her as an extra crew member when he brought my old Hatteras yacht-fisherman up to the Chesapeake Bay after I bought *Bayside*. Then he met Lindsay up here, and conveniently forgot to mention to her about Dawn and the fact that they were engaged by then. He lost both women as well as his job in the span of one morning. Somehow he managed to wear Lindsay down and get her back, and they've been together for the past three years. Dawn and I quickly figured out that we were meant to be together, too. It's funny the way things work out sometimes if you just let them.

As the Fates would have it, the four of us ended up fishing some high-dollar tournaments against each other, and all of us had our share of wins. Somewhere along the way Murph and I mended fences. Okay, there was rum involved. Enough rum that Lindsay and Dawn figured out they had a lot more in common than just Murph, and they became fast friends. Yes, that took quite a bit of rum. When the dust settled and our heads cleared we decided to get into some real estate deals together, starting with *Mallard Cove*. Murph and Lindsay had just put a contract on the property, but didn't know exactly what to do with it yet. Dawn and I had the capital to renovate and expand it, plus we had Kari and her winning plan for the property. And it has become quite a home-run.

So, Dawn tolerates Murph now. If he hadn't two-timed her, she and I'd have never gotten together, and she would never have met her best female friend. So, we're all four involved along with some other partners in *Mallard Cove*, *Lynnhaven*, and now *Cape Charles*, if in fact, we end up with this deal.

WE MET at the coffee house in Cape Charles for lunch and received quite a welcome. Or, I should say that Lindsay and Murph got quite a welcome from the wait staff and the owner. I had forgotten they spent some time here on the boat they lived aboard before they moved it to *Mallard Cove*. Apparently, the two of them had become favorites when they were here, and that added another point in our favor. They explained why they were in town, and who Dawn, Kari, and I were. By the time we finished our meal, there were some glances in our direction from a few of the other tables as the word spread. The development of the rail yards was the biggest news of the year so far and we were a hot item, just as I'd hoped.

After lunch, we went across the street to the rail yards to walk

Murph and Lindsay through the plan. If you want attention, take a roll of blueprints with you to a vacant piece of property, that'll do it. Sure enough, as we finished up and walked back to Mason Avenue, Robert Shalloway was headed straight for us, looking like we were playing with his favorite toy without permission. The ESVA Telegraph wires must've already been humming.

Shalloway shouted, "You can't just come over here and trespass whenever you want to! If you need access to that property, you have to call the town hall and arrange it first."

I've seen his type so many times, a tiny bit of power going straight to his head. This was a pivotal point. If I let him berate us here on the sidewalk, and we end up getting the project, he'd be able to continually bully us. Already a few folks had stopped and were staring.

"Gee, Bobby, I didn't realize you had to come over and unlock the place for us," I replied, in my most condescending tone.

"It's Mayor Shalloway, and that's town property, so yes, you do need my permission!"

Lindsay asked loudly, "Does your brother-in-law, Glenn Cetta have to get permission, too? Or, does he have free run of the place since he's your business partner?" She quickly lowered her voice so only Shalloway and our group could hear, "By the way, tell him Lindsay Davis said hello, and that I'm really enjoying that houseboat he gave me. Everything I had to do to get it was well worth it. Tell him that I'm sorry, I know he wanted to play rough, but I hope the bruises on his butt faded fast. I know it must've been tough to sit down for a few days, but after all, it was his idea. Probably was even tougher to explain that to your sister though, I hope he had a good excuse ready. But it's not my fault he's so kinky."

Lindsay calling him out loudly for being Cetta's not-so-secret partner was bad enough. That by itself would have made him explode and try to defend himself if she had just left it at that. But by switching tactics and accusing his sister's husband of infidelity, then including just enough truth to make it seem plausible overloaded Cetta's comprehension capabilities. His jaw worked up and down a few times, but no sound came out. His forehead furrowed and a vein started throbbing in his neck. Maybe he had heard that Cetta had cut someone a deep discount to get rid of that houseboat, or maybe he recalled back when his brother-in-law had to be very careful about sitting down, but in any case, some kernel of truth clicked with him. At this point, Shalloway's "big brother instinct" for protecting his sister kicked in, and he silently turned on his heel. He was in a hurry to call his sister's husband for some answers, but he wanted to do it from the privacy of his office.

To the locals on the sidewalk who hadn't heard the personal comments, it looked like Shalloway had run away after having been outed as his brother-in-law's development partner. Certainly not a great look for a politician, and something that wouldn't take long to get those telegraph wires humming again. Lindsay looked very pleased with herself.

I said, "You harlot!"

She laughed. "Okay, he didn't quite *give* us that houseboat, but it was close. And as far as what we had to do to get it, dragging it back across the Chesapeake was a chore. And who knows, the guy may be kinky. At the very least he's creepy! I bet that's a humdinger of a conversation he and his bro-in-law are having right now."

The rest of us joined her in laughing about it. There's nothing quite as satisfying as turning the tables on a narcissist like Shalloway. The fun now over, we went back to what we came here for. We browsed through a couple of shops and had just emerged from a bakery when we ran into Shalloway again, and he was furious.

He pointed a finger in Lindsay's face, "You're just lucky that you're not in jail! If you'd have hit me with a sinker, that's where you'd still be. Glenn's far more forgiving than I am. And you need to watch what you say about him, accusing him of sleeping with you."

Dawn defended her friend, "She never said that, you just assumed he did. And are you sure it was a sinker?" Shalloway now stuck a finger in her face, which she batted away. Now he pushed Dawn, and that was it, I shoved him backward and he lost his balance, landing flat on his butt.

"Do not *ever* touch her again, or you'll be very, very sorry, do you understand me?" He glared at me from down on the concrete but was smart enough to stay where he was. If he had tried to get up, I would have laid him out.

While he knew enough to stay down, he wasn't smart enough to shut up. "This is my town, and if you think you can come in here and steal that property away, you've got another thing coming. Both Markham and Withers are in for a rude awakening if they think they've got this thing in the bag."

Maybe he knew something that we didn't, or maybe he was pulling the same psych-out that Lindsay had. One thing was certain, he really looked stupid trying to threaten us while still sitting on the sidewalk. And I wasn't going to let his threat go unchallenged, especially since we now had a small crowd around us.

"I don't know who has what in a bag. I can tell you this, we didn't come here to 'steal' anything. We're going to let our proposal speak for itself. Everything about ours is out in the open, including the list of all our partners, which is more than your brother-in-law can say. Just remember this, Shalloway, don't you ever try to lay a hand on any one of us again, or you'll pay dearly for it."

CASEY AND KARI had been so intent on Shalloway, they never noticed the Richmond lawyer in the crowd. The town hall receptionist had pointed him in this direction when he had come in asking for more information. She had said that only the mayor could help him, and he might be able to catch him if he hurried. But now he had even more than he came for, and his client would be pleased.

HALF AN HOUR later in the tackle shop, the owner smiled and introduced himself to me and said hello to Murph. We had split off from the women, leaving them to browse other shops while we went into this place that was much more suited to our comfort level. The owner shook my hand. "I heard you knocked Shalloway flat out, and told him you were gonna kill him if he looked crossways at you."

That caught me off-guard. "Not really. He shoved my girlfriend, so I shoved him on his butt; I didn't hit him. And I just warned him not to touch any of us again."

"Un huh. Well, whatever you said or did, it was about time that somebody did it. That boy's a first-class jerk."

I nodded as Murph asked, "How did he get to be mayor, anyway?"

"Same way we get so many idiots in all them public offices. Not enough of the good people get off their duffs an' vote, the only research they do is count yard signs or listen to political ads. So we only end up with a list of egomaniacs to choose from. Shalloway got elected in an off-year; there wasn't much else goin' on. He's stayed there the same way all of 'em stay, 'cause people don't pay attention to what's happenin'. They get in the booth and think 'oh, I've heard a him' even though they can't recall if it was good or bad. Remember when we was kids the newspaper always printed the votin' list a week or so ahead a time so's you could figure it out? None of today's kids read newspapers, so they don't even bother printin' the list no more."

I shook my head sadly, "I wish they would start, otherwise we'll end up with a bunch of Shalloways running the world."

He nodded. "They already are."

After buying a new lightweight bait rod for myself, and Murph getting some new lures, we headed over to the distillery where we had agreed to meet Dawn, Lindsay, and Kari. Fortunately, we were early, and hopefully they would be late. I liked the looks of this place. As we walked through the door a pretty redhead came out from behind the counter.

"Murph! I haven't seen you in ages!" She hugged him and then looked over at me. "And you must be that Casey Shaw fellow I've been hearing so much about. I'm Lucy and welcome to Chuck's Distillery. Did you really knock the mayor out and bust his two front teeth?"

"Um, no. I just shoved him after he shoved my fiancée. The only part of him that got hurt was his rear end and his pride." It sounds like if I hang around any longer, the next person I meet will have heard that Shalloway is on life support.

"Well, I wish I had been there to see it happen. I'm glad you came in and dragged this dock rat back here with you. Your 'tasting' is on the house, Mr. Shaw."

I said, "Please call me Casey, Lucy."

"Casey it is then."

Murph protested, "What about another free tasting for old times' sake, Lucy?"

Lucy winked and said, "Sorry sweetie. Maybe if there had been some 'old times' I'd have comped yours, too. But did you forget already that you passed on your free shot when you got hooked up with that blonde instead of me? I just heard she's back in town, too."

I looked at him as he gave me half a shrug. I knew there was more to the story, but I also knew better than to ask. He had come straight down here after leaving *Bayside*. At that point Lindsay still wanted him dead, so he had been a free agent. Now seeing how pretty this woman is and hearing that Murph had turned her down, he must have already figured out that his future was with Lindsay by the time he got to town. Good to know, because he had been quite a "player" back in Florida, and this lady would have been right up his alley back then. Murph changed a lot when he got to ESVA, most of it for the better.

Lucy said, "So, are you a 'rummie' like Murph here, or are you more into vodka or bourbon?"

I replied, "Normally rum, though I've taken up vodka on the rocks lately."

"Perfect! Step into my office, gentlemen." She swept her arm toward some tall chairs in front of an empty tasting bar before she walked around the back.

I only like certain vodkas, but after tasting hers the list had now gotten longer. It was as smooth as any I'd ever had and almost as sweet as rainwater. She kept putting small tasting glasses in front of me, the contents running the gamut from rum to bourbon and even as far as flavored Virginia moonshines. Everything was excellent, there wasn't a single one that I'd turn down. But when it came time to pick one for a full-sized drink, I went with the vodka.

Lucy reached down into a freezer and pulled out a frosty bottle. "Be careful with these, Casey. Just because they taste like water, they don't *act* like it. And you can get this at all the restaurants in town that have full bars."

By the time I finished my second one, I realized I was through making my rounds for the day; this stuff was deceivingly potent. Murph had a two-rum smile going as well.

"I thought we were all supposed to be working!"

I turned and saw a bemused Dawn standing behind me. "Your fault."

She raised her eyebrows, "How can it be my fault?"

I grinned while handing her my car keys. "By showing up after I've had a second drink."

"Two drinks and you're already handing me your keys? Did you 'down' those things or are you becoming a wimp in your old age," she asked.

"You haven't tried this stuff yet." I looked past Dawn over to Kari, "I'm sending you home with some of this vodka for Marlin. It rivals that stuff he and his... uncle used to drink." I almost slipped and said something else, something we all knew, but agreed to never talk about. One of those stories from another day.

"Okayyyyy?" She tilted her head slightly, in a questioning manner.

I waved her over and handed her my glass. One sip and she understood saying, "And Marlin may even end up getting some of it."

Murph asked, "Just to be clear, we're still talking about vodka, right? Ow!" Lindsay had slapped the back of his head.

"You can be such a child at times," Lindsay accused him.

Kari winked at Murph as she passed my glass back to me. "Maybe, Murph."

"Jeeze, Kari, don't encourage him." Lindsay grabbed my glass before I had a chance to have another sip. "Oh hey, that's nice!

"Boys, how about un-assing those chairs and letting us women have a chance," Dawn said.

I got down off the chair, but not before motioning for another round for Murph and me.

The women took their time working through their array of spirits while joking with Lucy. Then we all left after another round of drinks, taking two cases of Chuck's finest with us.

5

THE INVITATION

I'd love to say those were my last drinks yesterday, but they weren't. While Murph, Lindsay, and Kari went home to their houseboats at *Mallard Cove*, Dawn and I returned to her floating namesake. We had a few more "Chuck's Martinis" as we named them up on the upper deck while we waited for the sun to set. It's been our "thing" for the past two years, ever since the first day we arrived here and watched that first sunset. By the time it disappeared over the Chesapeake, we were both feeling no pain. That Chuck's vodka was some dangerous stuff. One good thing about it though is that despite having over-served ourselves, neither of us had much in the way of a hangover today. I think I have a new favorite drink.

Having made our presence well known in Cape Charles yesterday, we decided to let the hornet's nest calm down for a day or two before going back. We still had over a week before the next council meeting when the Jersey contingent was going to present their plan, so there was plenty of time to show our faces again. Plus, I had quite a list to take care of before I could break away again during the day.

~

THE FOUR ARRIVED in Cape Charles a little after sunup and split into two couples that each went different directions, having breakfast in two different places. They wanted to get the lay of the land as quickly as possible. Then one pair would head for *Bayside* while the other two stayed put. But this was ground zero, the place where according to the information they'd been given, all their targets should show in the next few days if everything went well. Then it was do the job and get out.

~

"GOT time for lunch over at *The Bluffs*, Case? My treat." The voice belonged to my second favorite woman in the world, Rikki Jenkins, and she was leaning in through my doorway.

I looked at my watch, surprised that the morning was almost gone. "I didn't realize what time it was already, Rik. Yeah, sure, let's go."

In the past, Rikki Jenkins had been somewhat of a chameleon, because of her job. She used to do fieldwork for her father's security agency, and frequently had to change her look. But since she bought him out and brought in a couple of partners, she's been relegated to the office at ESVA Security, which occupies the far end of our single-story office building here at *Bayside*. Rikki's 5'-9" tall, in her early thirties, nicely built, with ice blue eyes and a short hairstyle in her natural platinum color. I'm glad she can pick her own look now without her job dictating what it needs to be.

ESVA Security has branched out under Rikki's direction. As the name suggests they do private security work, supplying temporary bodyguards and the like. But that's a small part of their business. Their main gig is stealthy contract work for the government. Stuff that no politico wants any government agency to touch, and few to know about. No paper trails, no connections to them. Jobs that command huge price tags in order to provide the two words that every politician loves to hear: "plausible deniability."

As I said before, *The Bluffs* was the second marina that I bought and renovated here on ESVA. It's on the Atlantic side of the peninsula, almost directly across from *Bayside*. It has a decent amount of land underneath its three small houses that are perched on a ridge overlooking the marina basin. We're just finishing up the installation of three sets of floating docks. When I bought it there was only a single rickety wooden pier on the north side of the basin. In the summer I keep my fifty-five-foot Jarrett Bay sportfisherman, *Predator*, docked here. We've got easy access to the Atlantic out of *The Bluffs*, and we converted one of the houses into a restaurant. Nothing as fancy as any of those at *Bayside*, which is just the way I like it. I wanted a casual place where any fishermen and most locals could afford to bring their families, yet enjoy food equal to the caliber of what we serve at *Bayside*. We nailed it.

I also hired an old Seminole friend from Florida, Noah Billie, to build a huge, authentic Seminole Indian chickee for the outside bar. In a concession to the Native American tribes, there are certain exemptions to building and zoning codes for work done, buildings built, and properties owned or leased by members of certified tribes. It was an extension of a treaty between the king of England and indigenous tribes back in the sixteen-hundreds.

I love this chickee, it reminds me of Florida, but it also reminds me that it was built with no permit or government permission needed. I've had enough run-ins with unscrupulous building inspectors and zoning officials throughout the years. Being able to thumb my nose at them by building this structure was too tempting, and it's now my favorite of all the bars we own. Rik and I took a table on the outside deck overlooking the marina, in the shade of the chickee.

"Jeff sure keeps *Predator* looking great," Rikki commented.

"Yeah, he was a great choice for captain. Which reminds me, we need to get out and fish soon."

She chuckled. "Twist my arm. We've both been so darn busy, I've forgotten how to hold a rod."

"I know, lots of irons in the fire. When I was a kid, living and working in that boatyard in Florida, I always wondered why the people who had such beautiful sportfishing rigs hardly ever used them. Their captains were continually bitching that their bosses never had any time to fish. Now I get it; they were working their tails off to be able to afford the boats. The irony of that is so thick. I always swore that if I ever got rich enough to afford one, I'd never let that happen to me. Hah!"

She cocked her head a little, "But you don't have to work as hard as you do, Case."

I looked out across the muddy grass flats that surrounded the basin. "If I didn't keep pushing, I wouldn't be me, you know that. This is what I do, this is who I am, Rik. Plus, I couldn't ask the people that work with me to work hard. It's also about setting an example. I think that's a big part of why we're friends, we're a lot alike in that respect."

Her reply was a silent nod. She and Dawn are the two women in my life that I am comfortable with being completely silent. Let me explain that a little better, I don't mean that I want or need them to shut up. I'm trying to say that we can be in the same room or fishing cockpit for hours on end together without feeling the need to fill the silence with meaningless talk or jabber. To know even one person like that is a gift. To know two is about as fortunate as you can get.

Our silence was broken by my phone. Larry Markham was calling. "Hey, Larry."

"Hey Casey. That was some show you put on down here yesterday."

"I didn't do it, Larry, your buddy Bobby did. It's not like I went looking for the guy. We were just down there to show interest in the town, and let everyone see that we're ESVA locals, even if only one of our partners is a 'born here.' But it sure seems like there are a lot of people who don't like your mayor."

I heard him laugh. "That's an understatement. Oh, and he hates being called Bobby, by the way."

"I know. I did it because he got under my skin. I wouldn't do it at a council meeting. But he came at me full bore, and I wanted to throw him off-kilter a bit." I didn't have to add that I wouldn't hesitate to do it again under similar circumstances. Larry already knew that.

"Oh, it worked. And whatever the blond woman said worked even better. He's still fuming, from what I hear. And speaking of hearing things, do you have time for dinner tonight at the *Shack*? There are a couple of things I'd like to go over with you in person. Mostly questions folks are asking me about you."

I didn't hesitate. "Sure. What time?"

"How about eight? We can use that same room, and most of the dinner crowd will have thinned out by then, we can have some privacy in public, if you know what I mean."

"I do. I'll see you there at eight." I hung up.

Rikki asked, "Trouble?"

"No. Probably just more of the same. One thing about small-town politics is that the politicians do have to be more responsive to their constituents since they see them more often and know a lot of them. I'll be happy to answer his questions so he can give answers right back to whoever asked him. Larry Markham is a good ally to have, and I want to do whatever I can to keep him happy."

"Speaking of happy, how's life these days? Seems like we're always talking about business, and lately just in passing," Rikki said.

"Life's good." I paused, a bit taken aback by the question. "I guess I've been pushing a bit too hard and we haven't spent much time together. I'm sorry about that, Rik."

She looked surprised. "Oh, I wasn't talking about us, although I always enjoy hanging together. I was thinking more along the lines of you and Dawn. Your divorce from Sally has been final for a while, and Dawn's been your fiancée through thick and thin. I figured you two would be making wedding plans by now."

If she had been anybody else, I'd have told her to butt out. But Rik's my pal, and she has jumped into the line of fire for me more than once. Literally. Between the two of us, we can say anything to each other without having to worry that we've overstepped our boundaries. We don't have any.

"I could say the same about you and Cindy you know." Cindy Crenshaw and Rikki have been together a few months longer than Dawn and me, and they live aboard their fifty-two foot Hatteras named *Hibiscus* at *Bayside*, right next to *Lady Dawn*. Cindy is a partner in all of our businesses. We originally brought her in to run our first hotel at Bayside, then realized that she could handle the whole resort. Then she and Kari designed the hotel at *Mallard Cove*, which led us to put her over all the hospitality and club operations. She's that sharp and has become a great friend as well.

"Oh, we've talked about it, but right now we're happy with things the way they are."

I was confused. "And you think Dawn isn't?"

"I think she would be happier if you two set a date." When I didn't reply right away she added, "It wouldn't have to be next week. But there's a certain amount of reassurance for her in that idea, Case."

The thing about Rikki is she always has my back. And she understands women more than me. Now she had me thinking, and I'll admit I'm worrying a bit, too.

"You think Cindy ever worries about... things, Rik?"

She laughed. "No. We did all the legal stuff a while back. In my line of work, well you know how it is. I wanted to make sure she was covered if something happened to me, and if medical decisions needed to be made about me, she could do those."

"Maybe Dawn and I should do that too."

"Not a bad idea, and a good first step if you intend on eventually getting married."

Well, this isn't the lunch conversation that I expected to have. But that's Rikki. She hits you with whatever is on her mind, and usually, it ends up being pretty timely. I texted my attorney and had an answer before we finished our meal.

I LEFT the office a little early, meeting Dawn at C3 for a swim and a drink since I was having dinner down at Cape Charles with Larry Markham. C3 is our private getaway clubhouse that we share with a handful of our friends. Set back in the woods beyond the marina parking lot, it's about as private as it gets with its own security fence and gate. Private enough for some to erase a tan line or two, but also a nice getaway from the demands of living where we work.

C3 has a hot tub and pool combination, outdoor kitchen with fire pit, and a "clubhouse" with a bar, sauna, pool table, fireplace, widescreen TV, and a glass wall that looks out over the pool and bay. You see, no matter how big your boat is, there's no having a pool table in it. The only other pool table I've ever owned I lost in my first divorce along with my first and only house. I've lived aboard boats ever since. C3 also has a killer view of the Chesapeake from the infinity pool and hot tub, even better than off the top deck of *Lady Dawn*.

Soaking in the hot tub with a glass of wine in one hand and Dawn's free hand in the other (she had a glass of wine too), I realized how much I loved this place, this life, and this woman.

"We need to set a date."

She said, "For what?"

"Um, our wedding?"

"I thought you wanted to wait a bit. It hasn't been that long since your divorce was finalized."

I was a little taken aback. "Change your mind?"

"No, I just want you to be sure. Need you to be sure."

"Trust me, I'm sure."

"Okay, let's do it next summer up in Oxford. There's a church there that generations of my family have been attending for over a hundred years. It's small, so that cuts the guest list down."

Guest list. Okay, this is about to get real. I saw her staring at me. "What?"

"You look shocked. We don't have to do this now, Casey."

I shook my head. "We're not. This is next year we're talking about."

"Un huh. For a guy who's been married twice, you sure have forgotten about all the prep work that goes into a wedding."

"Well then, we could make it easier and elope."

"Or not. Church. Family church. Hundred years. What part of all that did you miss?"

I couldn't tell if she was amused or annoyed. Probably the latter.

See, I'm in my element when it comes to business and boats. Women and relationships? Not so much. "I just wanted to give you options."

"Understood and appreciated. Church."

"Also understood. Church. And in the meantime, we have some documents to sign."

She tilted her head, "What kind of documents?"

I said, "Power of Attorney, Living Will, regular Will, Estate Trust Update, those things. Right now, legally, I have no one to take over decisions for me if I'm incapacitated, and I want you to be able to. Plus, I want to take care of you in case something happens to me between now and when we get married."

"Something going on that I should know about?"

I shook my head. "No, this is just stuff I should have done a while ago. I'm sorry it has taken so long."

She set her wine down, wrapped her arms around me, and kissed me. Leaning back and looking into my eyes she said, "Don't let anything happen to you, Casey."

I laughed. "Not planning on it. Kind of hard to get in trouble building marinas and buildings."

"Yet you have in the past." She looked concerned.

"That was then, this is now. No more trouble. Just boring building," I smiled. But I swear I heard the Fates laughing.

6

THE GAP

N *orthampton, VA, present-day...*

I was taken into a small interrogation room and made to sit in a metal chair, my hands now cuffed in front of me. A stone-faced detective came in, taking a seat across the table. He had a notebook and a plastic evidence bag with what appeared to be my wallet sealed inside.

"Mr. Shaw, I'm Detective Lonnano. Would you like to tell me what happened last night at the beach?"

"At the what?"

"Cape Charles beach. You were there last night, it's where you murdered Mayor Shalloway."

"I wasn't at the beach last night." Of the bits and pieces of memory that I could put together from last night, none of it was from the beach. It was all centered around the *Shack*, and I had no recollection of ever seeing Shalloway.

Lonnano had on his best poker face as he held the bag up so that I could identify the contents. "Is this your wallet, Mr. Shaw?"

There was no mistaking my *Rednecks and Radicals* wallet. They're not that common, and they have a deep logo imprint in the leather. Mine also has a mark above the logo where Murph hooked the wallet. We were fishing in the middle of an insane mahi run last year and he was trying to pitch another bait out quickly, but snagged me instead. The thick leather literally saved my... pride.

"It looks like it might be."

"It contains your identification, concealed carry permit, credit cards, and twenty-two dollars in cash."

"Like I said, it looks like it might be."

"Well, I think we can assume that it is. And if you weren't at the beach last night, then why was your wallet there? It was found under the body of Robert Shalloway, who had been impaled on a broken end of a snow fence."

"I have no idea how it got there, but I wasn't at the beach."

"Then where were you last night?"

"I had dinner with council member Markham at the *Shack*."

"What time was that?"

"We met there around eight."

"What time did you and the council member leave?"

"I'm not certain. Maybe an hour or so later?"

"So, you left together?"

"I don't recall. I may have gone to the head before leaving."

"Then you went to the beach to meet Mayor Shalloway."

He was starting to get under my skin.

"No! I went home."

"No, you texted the mayor and asked him to meet you at the pavilion at nine-thirty, telling him you wanted to settle the deal over the rail yard property."

"What? No! I never texted him."

"That's not what his phone shows. And he died sometime between nine-thirty and ten p.m. And now we have your phone, which will confirm you texted him." He held up another bag, with my smartphone in it. "I'll need you to unlock it for me."

"I think I'll pass. In fact, I think I'm through talking until I get a lawyer."

As I finished saying that, there was the sound of a heavy helicopter arriving outside. If I had to guess, I'd say it sounded like Eric Clarke's Sikorsky S-76. Eric is a friend as well as a board member and partner in *Bayside* and is building the first house in *Bayside Estates*. I had heard him making a call as I was led out of our conference room earlier, probably already arranging for a lawyer. As the multi-billionaire owner of an organic food business in northern Virginia, Eric has a lot of pull around the commonwealth. My hunch proved correct, as my new defense attorney walked into the room three minutes later.

"I'm Howard Falcon, Mr. Shaw's attorney. Mr. Shaw, don't say another word."

Lonnano looked smug. "He don't have to, he already admitted being in the area where the murder happened."

"I did not! I said I had dinner at the *Shack*, and said I wasn't anywhere near the beach."

"Yeah, well, the *Shack* is close enough; it's only a five-minute walk from there," Lonnano said.

This guy was an idiot. "The whole town is only a five-minute walk from there! That's why they built the pavilion where they did."

"How did you know the body was found by the pavilion?" Lonnano's look went from smug to triumphant.

"You said he got a text asking him to meet me there! You said that Shalloway was murdered on the beach on a snow fence. Last time I looked, the pavilion was at the beach, and there are snow fences all over the dunes. Duh!"

"Enough! Detective, I want to confer with my client in private. Please leave, and turn off all recording and listening devices," Falcon asked.

Lonnano glared at me as he left. Falcon waited until the red light on the camera by the ceiling went out before talking. He reached a hand across the table, and I shook it as best as I could, with both of mine still shackled together.

"Howard Falcon, nice to meet you Mr. Shaw. Eric Clarke retained me to act as your defense attorney."

"Call me Casey. I figured that was his helicopter I heard landing."

"It was the fastest way for me to get here from Richmond, and I don't think they expected you to have an attorney in place for quite a while. Okay, Casey, tell me everything you remember about last night, then everything that detective asked, and what you said to him."

Falcon took a legal pad out of his briefcase and began taking notes as I slowly went through every detail I could recall, including Dawn finding out about the ride-share. When I finished, he sighed.

"So, we have roughly a two-hour and thirty-minute gap where you have no recollection of what happened. We need to fill in that gap."

There was a rap on the door, and the detective barged in, holding the bag with my phone and a sheet of paper. "This is a search warrant requiring you to open this phone." He looked more smug than ever as Falcon took the warrant from him. Then he looked over at me and nodded. I used the facial recognition feature to unlock it, then handed it to him. He tapped the screen a couple of times and said, "So, you didn't text the mayor last night, eh? I suppose this phone is so smart it did it by itself! And we have half a dozen witnesses who will swear that you threatened the mayor outside the bakery the day before he was murdered."

Lonnano held the screen up for both Falcon and me to read. It showed that the text asking Shalloway to come to the pavilion had indeed come from my phone. But I had no idea how that got on there. I didn't send it, I couldn't have. That might make the rest of this nightmare true. Why couldn't I remember anything during those two hours?

MY NEXT FEW hours were also a blur. In the middle of the afternoon I was arraigned at the courthouse with Howard Falcon at my side, representing me. The prosecutor wanted me held without bail, claiming I was a flight risk since I have my own airplanes, boats, and access to cash. Howard countered with my strong ties to the ESVA community and got the judge to agree to two-million in bail, plus I had to surrender my passport, and I'm not to travel outside of Virginia. To ensure that, I have to wear an electronic ankle monitor. Dawn was in the gallery waiting on the outcome and arranged for the bail.

I knew the local press would be all over this, and maybe even the VA Beach television news, but I hadn't counted on such a large press gaggle waiting outside. Because *Bayside* has such a high profile with the Richmond and DC crowds, their news crews were represented as well. That wasn't good. I knew that the local news would associate me with McAlister and Shaw development, and that was bad enough. But connecting me with the resort and the club and having this in the news of our two biggest target areas will be a complete public relations disaster.

Howard made a statement for the reporters, "My client is innocent, and we intend to prove that in court."

A blond tv reporter with big hair shouted, "Is it true that he threatened to kill Mayor Shalloway the day before he was murdered?"

"At no time did my client ever threaten to kill Mayor Shalloway."

Another asked, "Isn't it true that Mr. Shaw hated Shalloway?"

"My client barely knew Mr. Shalloway, and had no reason to want to hurt him."

The first reporter persisted, "But several witnesses have said he knocked Shalloway to the ground the day before."

"That statement is incorrect. The truth will come out at the trial, where I'm certain Mr. Shaw will be acquitted. That's all we have to say for now."

THE THREE OF us climbed into Dawn's Escalade and headed north to *Bayside*. Once there we passed through the security fence at the south dock parking area which will keep any reporters out. We went aboard *Lady Dawn* where Eric, Rikki, and Cindy were all waiting for us in the salon. I introduced Falcon, and his eyebrows raised when I got to Rikki.

"I've heard of you and your company," he said. "Very impressive."

Rikki shrugged, "I can say the same about you. Now let's hope that together we can keep Case out of jail."

"Together?" Falcon asked.

"Whatever you need intelligence-wise, we'll be happy to provide. We've got friends in a lot of places, including the state police crime lab, where they've taken Casey's Cherokee."

That surprised me since I figured it was still in the parking lot of the *Shack* right where I'd left it. "Why'd they take my Jeep?"

Falcon answered, "They're not missing a trick. Probably looking for clues that can tie you to the pavilion area."

"I didn't kill the man, I wasn't at the beach, and there's nothing to tie me to the pavilion!"

"All true, but we have a two and a half hour void to fill in so we can prove that," Falcon said.

"Case, the even bigger point is that somebody is doing a damn good job of framing you for murder. We need to figure out why, and that'll help us figure out who. Then we have to prove it." Rikki had her determined look on her face, and it made me feel a little better until Cindy spoke up.

"Uh, oh. That's not good." Cindy was looking through the window across the marina basin. At the end of one of the docks that pesky reporter from back at the courthouse was now doing a "standup" with *Lady Dawn* in the background.

I followed her gaze and said, "Can we get someone over there to chase them off?"

Cindy replied, "We can, if you want to make it an even bigger story. It's too late now, they've already got their shot."

"Casey, I hate to say this, but we need to get you out of here, minimize your linkage to Bayside, and do some damage control. If you're not here where you can be found and seen, that'll help," Eric suggested. "You and Dawn have become synonymous with *Bayside*, and the public now thinks one of you murdered someone. Bayside needs to become divorced from you two, at least until this blows over and we can prove you're innocent."

I glanced at Dawn, who nodded gently and said, "Eric's right, we need to move the boat out of *Bayside*. We can go to *Mallard Cove* and work out of there for a while until things settle down."

I looked over at Cindy, and I didn't have to ask her opinion. I could see the sadness on her face. I nodded to her and said, "*Bayside*, the *Estates,* and the *Club* are all in your hands now."

"I've got this, Casey."

"I knew you could handle it from day one, Cindy." Before she came to work here, she had been with a corporation that wasn't good at seeing the full abilities of the people they employ. I was never more grateful for that and for her than right now. The sadness I had seen on her face was now partially replaced by pride.

I said, "Eric, you're so well known, and we need to get back out in front of this thing before we start losing business. Would you be willing to become the Chairman of the *Bayside* related companies if I step down? A press release stating that could soothe and reassure our present and future clientele, especially those who already have or might be thinking about signing contracts to build homes here." His own home design on the premier lot on the point had set the tone for the others that are being built. Him putting down roots here was a big selling point with the DC crowd.

He answered, "I'll be happy to step in for as long as you want or need me to. That's a big step, and a big sacrifice by you, Casey. As a shareholder, I appreciate what you're willing to do to protect my investment. As a friend, it makes me admire you even more."

I nodded grimly. "Thanks, but you'd do the same thing, Eric. Every one of us in this room would. Let's get a press release out right away, so it gets included in any news report this evening. And we'll get out of here this afternoon."

7

MOVING DAY

Dawn, Bimini, and I were sitting on the afterdeck of *Lady Dawn* as our crew took her out of *Bayside* an hour before sunset. We had a little more than a two-hour Chesapeake cruise ahead to reach the tip of ESVA and *Mallard Cove*. We timed it so that our arrival would be after dark, hopefully drawing as little attention as possible.

Once everyone else had gone I was finally able to get some thinking done. With as crazy as it had been all day, and how bad I had felt this morning, everything had been a blur up until that point. Fortunately, I had a team I could trust, and friends who believed in my innocence. At least I hope they still do. And our boat's crew members were also in my corner. Not because I'm their boss, but because they're around Dawn and me so much each and every day. They know me and Dawn well, and how much strain we are under right now. They're giving us some space, mostly staying out of sight and leaving us to our thoughts. Without a doubt, we have the best crew on the water.

Watching *Bayside* disappearing astern was one of the saddest moments of my life. When I arrived here two winters ago it was a dilapidated wreck, and my team and I have turned it into the gem of ESVA in record time. It's the biggest and best project that I've completed to date. I just hope and pray that my association with it now doesn't bring its success to an end.

I've got to be able to prove my innocence, but even if I do, there's been damage to my companies and my reputation that will never be undone. You get accused of a brutal murder, and it's on page one. You get acquitted or the charges get dropped, and that's printed somewhere back by the classified section. Cindy, Eric, and Dawn also have investments in *Bayside* that I have to protect, and depending on what happens, it will probably mean my having to sell all my shares in that property to protect theirs. While that sounds easy, to me it would be like cutting off my own arm, but I'll do it to protect my friends. I love what we've accomplished together, the life we carved out for ourselves there, and the privacy we've enjoyed at C3. The idea of leaving that even for a short time is tough. Leaving it permanently I know would be something I'd never get over, but it's looking like it may come to that.

Bimini is one of the smartest dogs I've ever known, and he knew something bad was going on. He hasn't left my side since I got back to the boat, even foregoing his favorite huge cow bone and dog bed. He's laying with his chin on my left shoe as a reminder that he's there for me. The three of us sitting together watching the ESVA coastline pass by should've been fun, but instead I felt like I was having to sneak away and hide. Because that's exactly what I was doing.

We also timed our departure so that it would be dark by the time we passed Cape Charles. I didn't want anyone onshore recognizing our boat as we cruised by. We saw the lights of the houses on Bay Avenue through the cuts in the dune as we passed by offshore. I knew it was near one of those cuts where Shalloway had met his end. And while my life had changed because of that, I knew mine wasn't the only one. Many of those residents of Bay Avenue probably didn't even lock their doors before last night, but I'm willing to bet they're all locked now. They're shaken and scared... of me. I feel a bit like Frankenstein's monster. So, now there are two places where I can't show my face, *Bayside* and Cape Charles.

. . .

WHILE OUR INVESTMENT group also has a big chunk of *Mallard Cove*, Murph and Lindsay are the majority owners, and we had "thrown in" with them after they had it under contract. They are the public "faces" of that property, so our being there wouldn't be as noticeable. At least, I hope not. We've deliberately let very few people know about our association with that property. Though we have the whole top floor of an intentionally nondescript three-story office building at the marina, we're only using less than half that floor's square footage so far. It's home to *M&S Partners*, our acquisition and development arm that Kari runs. Now, at least temporarily, it'll also be home to *McAlister & Shaw*.

The second floor of the building is occupied by the *Mid-Atlantic Fishing Foundation* and their television production group, *Tuna Hunter Productions*. Plus the offices of the *Pelican Fleet*, which runs eco-tours, a parasail boat, a large sailing head boat, and a fleet of small rental catamarans at *Mallard Cove*. All of this is either run or owned by Marlin Denton, my good friend and now Kari's husband.

The first floor of the building is a parking garage. This is where the crew parked Dawn's Escalade when they shuttled it down here, and where my Jeep will go once it's released by the cops. It's much better hiding the cars in there than advertising our movements by parking next to the dock for everybody else to see if we're home or not. I want and need to keep as low a profile as possible.

We tied up to the end of the farthest east dock, our stern facing away from the *Cove's* restaurants and bars. *Lady Dawn* is the largest boat in the marina right now, and there's no sense drawing more attention than necessary by having her name easily seen by the diners at *Mallard Cove Restaurant* behind charter boat row. No doubt word would get out around the waterfront about where we relocated, but I'm not so concerned about boat owners and crews knowing that as I am with reporters. Unfortunately, *Lady Dawn* is too big to fit on the private dock here that's fenced off from the public. So right now anyone can walk up next to her. And we no longer have C3 adjacent to us for a private place to get out of public view and decompress, something that I could use right about now.

Since we planned to sneak in quietly under cover of darkness, I wasn't prepared for the size of the welcoming committee that was awaiting us. Andrea and Jeff from our crew I knew would already be there. They'll handle the dock lines since they went ahead to shuttle some of the cars down, but there was also a small crowd standing on the dock with them. As soon as the gangway was in place, Rikki came aboard with someone I hadn't seen before who had a medical bag in hand. Behind those two were Murph, Lindsay, Kari, Marlin, and Captain Bill "Baloney" Cooper.

Rikki and the doctor who accompanied her quickly ushered me down to the forward VIP guest stateroom, leaving Dawn with the rest of the group. On the way Rikki said, "Sorry, Case, I should have thought of this and had your blood drawn as soon as I heard you had a blank spot to fill in. We're going to take blood and urine, plus do a DNA swab because there've been a few developments. By the way, this is Dr. Stewart, he was suggested by Howard Falcon. He's been an expert witness in a lot of high profile cases."

Doing a full fluid profile suggested that there was something they were specifically looking for. I knew that Rik would get around to explaining what it was, but right now they were more intent on getting the samples asap before my body could filter out any more of what I'm assuming must be chemicals or drugs. Everything had to be sealed and signed by the doc, and he even went into the head to observe as I peed in the specimen cup. He apologized for the lack of privacy, but said he needed to be able to swear in court as to the origination and chain of custody of each sample. Back in the stateroom I sat on the edge of the bed as he did a DNA mouth swab. Once all the samples were taken he left, headed back to his lab to get started on the tests. Falcon had told him to put a rush on the results. Rik and I went to the salon, where my friends were waiting.

Baloney hopped to his feet and grabbed my hand to shake it. "Casey, I wanted you to know that I'm behind ya all the way. Hell, all of us here at the *Cove* are, we know you, an' that you're innocent. We got your back, a hundred percent."

If it weren't for the sincere and concerned look on his face, I might have smiled. Bill is as much a character as he is a friend. Just over fifty years old, and despite almost three decades of living on ESVA, he hasn't lost his native New Jersey accent, although he thinks he has. His ever-present cheap cigar hung from the corner of his mouth, unlit as usual. He and his wife Betty live aboard their salvaged fifty-four-foot Viking sportfish, *My Mahi*. Betty has a strict rule about Bill's cigars, they can only be lit after *Mahi* clears the marina bulkhead on the way out to fish. Having been downwind of a lit one on more than one occasion, it's a rule I'm glad she made. And in addition to being a charter boat captain, Bill recently became the highest-paid cast member of MAFF's top-rated cable reality show, *Tuna Hunters*.

"Thanks, Bill, that means a lot. I was hoping that would be the case, and it's part of why we decided to come here."

"Youse two here permanently now, or what?"

"Bill, right now I don't know what's permanent. Unless I can clear my name and find out who's trying to frame me, well, I don't know what's going to happen."

"Well, whatever you need from me, all ya gotta do is ask. I wanted to let you know I'll help ya any way I can. But I gotta go, I've got an all-day offshore charter tomorrow." He reached out his hand and I shook it again. Bill might be a bit overbearing, but you can always depend on him when things get tough. I saw the concern for me in his eyes, and it was humbling. After he left, I realized he hadn't even bummed a beer. He always mooches beer. It was yet another sign of how sincere and worried he is right now.

I went over and sat next to Dawn on one of the couches. The rest of the gang sat close by as Rikki brought us all up to date.

"I've got a friend over at the state's lab where they took your truck. I've got good news and bad news. The bad news is they found a bunch of fresh beach sand in your driver side floor mat."

That didn't make sense. "How would I have tracked in a pile of beach sand if I walked all the way from the pavilion through the grassy rail yard and across the *Shack's* gravel parking lot?"

She had a triumphant grin on her face, "That's part of the good news, you wouldn't have, or couldn't have. Unless you had driven over to the pavilion, gone out onto the beach, and then driven back to that parking lot."

I argued, "That doesn't make any sense. If I did that, why drive back to the restaurant? Why not go straight back home?"

She held up a hand, "Exactly, but wait, there's more. They found some vomit in the back passenger doorframe of your Cherokee. The vomit had traces of rohypnol, the 'date rape drug,' as well as ether in it. Two of my team went to the *Shack* to talk to the wait staff to see if they remembered you, and if they saw you leave, but instead what they found was a mess. A busboy was just about to hose down a pile of puke in the parking lot. We were able to get a sample of it, and now we need to match it to your DNA and do a chemical analysis."

Rik paused a minute and saw we were all hanging on what she was saying. "In talking to the kid, he said it must not have come from your Jeep because the state guys had hauled it off from the other side of the lot. So, unless two people puked there last night, your Jeep was moved, and whoever puked was in the back seat.

"When they got it to the lab they dusted the steering wheel, door handles, and shift knob for fingerprints, but everything had been wiped clean. There weren't even any of your prints on those surfaces.

"Then they went to find the restaurant owner and found him watching over a guy who was replacing the glass in the front door. It turns out the place got burglarized last night, sometime after midnight. The only thing that was taken was the video recorder from the security system. Those cameras cover the inside of the restaurant as well as the parking lot."

"Nothing else was missing?" I asked.

"Zip. Then they showed your picture to the bartender who had been on last night, he said he remembered you leaving with a middle-aged couple who said they were your friends. They had to hold you up on both sides since you were so out of it when you stumbled out of the head. He was surprised because he only sent two drinks each to you and Markham in the private room: scotch for him and vodka for you. So the bartender figured you must've had quite a few before you got there, even though he hadn't noticed you staggering when you came in."

I said, "I only had one wine in the pool with Dawn before I drove down there, that much I do remember clearly. And I didn't meet any friends there that I can remember."

Rikki continued, "The bartender started worrying about having over-served you, getting snagged by the Alcohol Beverage Control and risking the restaurant's license.

"That couple stood out to him because they picked the two stools next to the bar's service area, and those are usually the last two seats that get taken because of all the waitstaff traffic. Plus, there had been plenty of the more prime seats open the whole time they were there. They also only had one drink each and nursed them for over an hour, then didn't even leave a tip when they took off with you. He figured they were going to come back in, but then they never did."

"I don't remember any of that, Rik."

"You wouldn't if you were 'roofied,' and I'm pretty sure you were."

I said, "Markham would've known I wasn't loaded when I came in."

"They talked with him. He was reluctant to say anything at first because he had bought into the idea of you murdering Shalloway. Then when they asked how you acted, he said you seemed completely sober at first, but by the end of your second drink, you were slurring your words and were starting to act plastered. When they suggested you could have been drugged, he agreed that it seemed possible."

"What about the ride-share driver?"

Rik nodded, "We checked him out, too. Solid driver, great record. He said if it wasn't for your two 'friends' pushing him into it and that hundred dollar tip, he probably wouldn't have let you in his car. I guess he's had to clean up after drunks on more than one occasion."

"He thought I was just wasted?"

"Yeah, and your friends convinced him that you were beyond the puking stage. They also gave him the keypad combination for the security gate at *Bayside*. By the time you got to the boat you had recovered enough to make it up the gangway by yourself."

"How the hell would they have had the keypad combination?" I asked.

"This was no happenstance frame job, there was some real planning behind it and no doubt some surveillance, too. Quite a few *Bayside* employees use that keypad daily, it wouldn't be hard to watch from a distance with a scope to get the code."

"So, they were spying on me at *Bayside*?"

"Absolutely. Which means we probably caught them on the surveillance cameras. We're running through the last couple of days' recordings now since we have their descriptions." Rikki had designed the security camera layout at *Bayside*.

"Which could explain how they knew where to find me at Cape Charles if they were following me," I said.

"Exactly."

"Now we just need to figure out why they killed Shalloway just to frame me."

Rikki said, "I've got a theory about that..." Her phone ringing interrupted that sentence. She glanced at the screen then answered the call. "Yes...Un huh...Interesting...Yeah, bounce me those, and see if we can find out where that car went. Let's get into the rental agency's tracker system. Thanks."

Rikki looked up, "I was about to say that I had a theory, but now it's a bit more than that." Her phone pinged, and she held it up so I could see. She flipped back and forth between two mugshots, a man and a woman. "Case, do you recognize these two?"

Something about them looked familiar, but it was a fuzzy recollection at best. "Maybe. I feel like I've seen them before, I just don't know where. Who are they?"

"He's a freelance leg breaker, and she's a hooker. We identified them through facial recognition after we spotted them on the camera footage at *Bayside*. They were hanging around the docks yesterday, and we picked them out after they matched the bartender's description of 'your friends'. They got into a rental car and followed you out of the resort when you left for Cape Charles. They also matched the description that the driver gave us of the couple who 'helped' you in the parking lot last night."

"So, they were the ones who killed Shalloway?"

"It's looking that way, though it was probably the guy, given his past. Like I said, I have a theory about that. What did you and Shalloway have in common?"

I said, "I'd like to think that we didn't have much at all in common. The man was a slimeball."

"Yes you did, just don't think too hard, it should be obvious."

"Thanks a lot, Rik."

Dawn spoke up, "No, Casey, she means we're after the same piece of property!"

How could I have missed that? I guess I'm still fuzzier than I realize. "Right, duh! I was thinking more about Cetta as the buyer, but you're right, Shalloway was going to be his 'silent' partner."

"And now that Shalloway is dead, there's no way that his sister would want her husband to get involved with a property she thinks got her brother killed," Dawn said.

Rikki nodded. "Exactly. You're out of the picture, Case, because everybody in town thinks you killed their mayor. Cetta's out because his wife's brother was murdered, and now that town and property will continually remind them of that. Which leaves only one buyer."

"The mysterious party who is busy on a job in New Jersey," I said.

Rik said, "And guess where the goon and the hooker are from, and where their car was rented?"

Now Murph chimed in. "I'll put five bucks on Jersey for the win. It's all circling back to there. But why is the rail yard worth killing over? I mean, it's got great potential, it's beautiful waterfront, but there are some similar properties along the Chesapeake. I just don't get it."

Rikki replied, "I said I had a theory about who killed Shalloway, not why that property would get him killed. So I'm with you, Murph, I don't know either. But our main objective is to get Casey off the hook, then we'll figure out what's so important about that parcel.

Now we just need that specimen analysis back, so if I'm right we can go have a talk with the Commonwealth Attorney and get these charges dropped."

Kari asked, "How will those results do that?"

"They should back up my theory. That the New Jersey couple 'roofied' Casey's second drink with just strong enough of a dose to make him unable to drive. That's something they could have easily done without drawing attention since they were sitting next to the service bar. Then they get him out to his Jeep, where they used ether to knock him out completely. But the combination of the two drugs and the alcohol made him sick and he vomited. They held him partly out the rear passenger door, and some got on the doorframe but the majority ended up in the parking lot. Both chemicals should show up in high concentrations in the sample we took from the lot.

"Then we compare that to the concentrations from the samples we took tonight. This should give us a time window for when he was doped, and show that he would have been too impaired to have possibly killed Shalloway. In fact, I'm willing to bet that if they test Shalloway's blood, they'll find ether there, too. Remember, Shalloway was only expecting Casey, not a couple that he didn't know. It wasn't that late, and not that unusual for someone to take a walk down by the beach.

"The woman was pretty enough to have distracted him, giving her partner time to hold a rag full of ether over his face from behind him. Then it would've been much easier and quieter to be able to drag an unconscious Shalloway down to the beach. At a little before ten p.m., there might've still been someone in the area, so the noise from a fight or big struggle would've attracted attention. With him out cold it would've also been easier to impale Shalloway on that loose snow fence picket like it had happened in a fight, then plant Casey's wallet under his body. Shalloway bleeds out silently, then the killer uses something to wipe out or distort his footprints on his way back to the Jeep.

They drive around long enough for Casey to start waking back up, then park the car back at the restaurant which is now closed. Call for a ride-share on Casey's phone, get him loaded into the car then disappear."

Lindsay asked, "But how would they get into Casey's phone?"

Ricky said, "Facial recognition, they just hold it in front of him. Then they can send the text to Shalloway, and open the ride-share app."

I realized I was unconsciously nodding my head. Her whole scenario made sense. I'm glad someone could think straight because I was still having a tough go of it. "I think you've nailed it, Rik. Now all we have to do is sell it to the Commonwealth Attorney, and get Lonnano to start looking for the real killer."

Rikki stood up. "I should know more in the morning after we get those test results back. Meanwhile, get some rest. You too, Dawn, you guys have been through the ringer today."

8

IT'S ALL ABOUT VOTES

Marlin and Kari followed Rikki out, but I could see that Murph and Lindsay weren't in a hurry to leave yet. I didn't mind, because having them here was a good distraction. If I try to go to sleep now I know I'll just lie there and run everything back through my head, over and over again.

"I want some fresh air. Let's all go to the upper deck." I'd had enough of enclosed spaces, especially after being forcibly confined for more than half the day, including much of it in a holding cell. The four of us and Bimini climbed the aft stairway to the top deck, which was designed for entertaining. Dawn poured two glasses of wine for Lindsay and her, then sat in a pair of chaise lounges. I grabbed a couple of Red Stripe beers for Murph and me, as I was in no way ready to have any hard liquor today.

I passed Murph his bottle and walked over to the railing, looking across the marina basin and toward the private and charter boat docks. Murph joined me and remarked, "This place has come a long way in a short time."

"Sure has." I was glad that he and Lindsay had let us partner up with them and do the build-out, that had worked well for all of us. "I just hope the media doesn't figure out that I'm here, and that I'm in with you on this place. I'm bad for business, you know."

In the low light I could see his head turn to face me. "Screw 'em, Case. *Bayside* has the snootier customers, not us. Nobody will care that you're here. Knowing this crowd, some of 'em will probably want to meet you, the rest won't give a darn.

"Case, I never really understood why you took to that *Bayside* bunch anyway. You never liked that type when we were back in Florida; you avoided all those highbrows like they were the plague. Yeah, your boats may have gotten bigger and fancier over the past few years, but that was all about comfort, never about ego. Hell, you still drive that same model of Cherokee, the square 'rolling brick' that they haven't made in over a decade."

"Hey! Don't pick on my truck. I like the older ones."

Murph laughed quietly. "That's my point. You never gave one damn about what people thought before *Bayside* became such a hit with the DC crowd. Now you're scared to death that they might not want to patronize some place because you're there? That tells me you're in the wrong place. Why not think about making this move permanent? I know all the gang down here would love to have you guys stay. Linds and me especially."

"Remember, where I'll be staying for the next few decades is still up in the air, Murph. That decision may not be left up to me."

"Don't be negative, pal. If I had to bet money Case, I'd put it on Rikki and her being able to sell that theory she came up with."

I silently looked around the marina and realized that I didn't feel out of place here in the least. I knew that Stu Lieberman's hundred-forty-foot Benetti, *Deb's Emerald*, is based here a lot of the summer on the next dock over, so *Lady Dawn* won't stick out so much since she's thirty feet shorter. If it turns out that we can't or shouldn't go back to *Bayside*, there are much worse places to be docked than here. Though I'd miss C3 and those sunsets across the Chesapeake from *Bayside*. *Mallard Cove* faces southeast, meaning we can get sunrises only part of the year, and I'm a sunset kind of guy anyway.

· · ·

LATER I LAY on my back in bed as Dawn crawled in beside me. There was barely enough light coming in through the dockside portholes to let me see the outline of her face as she lay on her side with an arm across my chest.

"Hey, it'll be okay Case, I think Rik's got it figured out."

"She's got most of it, though we still need to fill in the remaining blanks. But I think, I *hope* we have enough to convince the Commonwealth Attorney that they've got the wrong guy."

"We do."

As I lay there, I could feel her watching me.

"Is that everything, Case? I mean, it's certainly enough, but it feels like there's something more. If it's the wedding, we can put that all on hold. In fact, we probably should put it on hold for now, that's the last thing you need to be worrying about."

"To be honest, I hadn't even thought about it, Dawn. I was thinking about something Murph said." I felt her stiffen a bit as I said it; old wounds never fully heal.

"What?"

"Before I tell you, let me ask you something. Are you happy at *Bayside*?"

"We built it."

"That's not what I asked you. I want to know if you are happy being docked at *Bayside*."

"On most days, yes. Though I'm glad we have C3 so that we can have some privacy when we want. At times it's like living in a fishbowl, especially after that article came out about us last year. So many people wanting our attention there now and that gets annoying at times. I wish we could get away from that but it's part of the price we pay for living there I guess. Why?"

"Murph pointed out a few things. The first was that the crowd at *Bayside* is like the crowd I went out of my way to avoid back in Florida. He said we won't draw much attention here, and I think he's right. He also said that the gang here would love to have us stay."

"So, you want to move away from *Bayside*?"

"Like I told him, I may not have the option of picking where I live for a long time."

Her arm tightened across my chest. "Don't say that!"

"We have to think about all the possibilities, Dawn."

"I'd rather think about all of our options, Casey, and you going to prison isn't one of them. Rik and Falcon will get this all straightened out, then we can figure out what we're going to do. But I'm not going to think about this until tomorrow, and you shouldn't either. I've got another idea for right now."

Dawn sat up and unbuttoned my oxford shirt she was using as a nightshirt, then let it drop onto the sheet. I liked her other idea.

AFTER TAKING Bim for a long post-kibble-breakfast walk, I saw Rikki was waiting for me in the salon. I couldn't read anything from her expression.

"Good morning Rik, I hope. Had breakfast yet?"

"Hours ago, Case. I didn't sleep well, I kept running things through my mind, over and over again. But you go ahead, I'll have some coffee and bring you up to date while you eat."

Walking into the galley we ran into Dawn, who was just coming upstairs. "Hi Rik, and good morning, Case."

The three of us sat at the crew table while our chef, Shauna, made Dawn and me breakfast. Rik took a sip of coffee then began.

"We had some good news and some bad news this morning. The good news being they found the rental car that the couple was using. It was in a field in Delaware, on the road that leads to the ferry. The bad news is that it was torched, and there were three bodies in it that had been shot before being set on fire."

"Three bodies?" Dawn asked.

Rik nodded. "Someone is tying up loose ends. I'm guessing there were two teams because somebody did the shooting and the burning. So three of them were expendable, and the remaining one was either whoever is behind all this, or was trusted enough to do the cleanup work for whoever is, and still live."

I was stunned. Whatever the reason for this has to be bigger than we thought. I mean, killing Shalloway was huge, but now the body count was climbing fast. "Sounds like they were heading back to New Jersey, if they were catching the ferry."

"Don't count on that last player heading back, Case, if that's where they're from. We don't know yet what this is all about, so we can't depend on anything more than we already know for certain. Two teams mean either twenty-four-hour surveillance, or they were watching two targets or two places. For all we know, that fourth person is already back in Cape Charles, since that seems to be the common denominator."

Rik handed me a phone like my old one. "I saw Kari on the way in, and she asked me to give you this. She loaded it from your cloud backup, but the new number is one digit higher than your old phone. She has a lot of different talents, doesn't she?"

"Really does. Glad she's on the team, especially since I'm side-lined. Cindy, too. With those two running everything I can concentrate on finding out what this is about, and who's behind it."

"You mean concentrate on clearing your name," Rikki said.

I replied, "Which can't happen completely until whoever is behind this gets identified and charged. Otherwise, it'll look like I bribed someone or I got off on a technicality but that I'm really guilty. Until somebody goes down for this, I'll never totally be cleared. To a lot of people, I'll never be cleared even *if* someone else is convicted."

Rik nodded, she knew who I meant. Then her phone rang. "Rikki... Yes... Dead on, that's great... Yeah, see you then." She hung up then looked at me.

"Falcon. He's on his way, should be here in an hour. The test results came back, and they were exactly what we thought. Doing a comparison of the samples, Doc Stewart was able to determine that you were roofied somewhere between eight and ten p.m. The timing of the ether wasn't as conclusive, other than it was present in the parking lot vomit.

"With these results, the identity of the two that were following you, the bartender and the ride-share driver's statements, the theft of the security recorder, plus the fact that no fingerprints were found, he thinks we have enough to convince the Commonwealth Attorney to drop the charges against you."

"He *thinks*? That damn sure better be enough! We're having to do all their work for them." Dawn was now what some of us who are close to her refer to as being "redhead pissed." Not something you want to be the focus of.

I said, "Lawyers, dear. You know how they always like to leave wiggle room. Don't worry, with all this new evidence, they'll have to drop the charges."

COMMONWEALTH ATTORNEY MICHAEL MARTINO SAID, "Nice theory, Mr. Falcon, but it doesn't exonerate your client. For all we know Mr. Shaw here has people following him around all the time that had nothing to do with Mayor Shalloway's murder. Maybe Mr. Shaw doped himself after he murdered Mayor Shalloway in order to create an alibi, and that whole drunken scene in the *Shack* was an act. Maybe he was the one who hired this so-called 'enforcer' and later murdered or had someone murder him. But that's Delaware's problem, not ours. Maybe you have friends up in their forensics lab just like you do here, and you'll find out before their investigators do, like what happened here." He had his nose way out of joint over that.

He continued, "What I know is this, I've got a live suspect who had means, motive, and opportunity, plus the fact that his wallet was found at the scene. And, there was sand that matches the crime scene in his car. The recorder at the *Shack* could have been stolen to cover the fact that your client drove back to the parking lot himself. There is no way I'm dropping the charges just because you have some wild alternative theory."

I said, "Especially in an election year, huh Martino? The truth doesn't matter until after all the ballots are cast, right?" I was hot, this guy was a political hack of the first order. Rikki grabbed my arm, she was sitting in a chair next to mine, and Falcon shot me a look from my other side that said, "Shut up!" I didn't care. This office should be about justice, not politics.

Lonnano was sitting across the conference table, glaring at me. "Yeah, well, I don't know how they do things up in Accomac county, but here in Northampton, we go by the book. The same book the judge is gonna throw at you. Enjoy that big yacht of yours at *Mallard Cove* for now, because after the trial's over things aren't gonna be as comfortable for you for say, the next twenty years?" He looked smug.

I guess I looked surprised that he knew I lived on a boat since I had only given the *Bayside* address, but he loved showing off. "That's right, hotshot, I know where you live, and where you just moved your boat to. I guess you forgot about that bit of ankle jewelry you're wearing. I know right where I can find you, whenever I want to, 24/7. And thanks for moving into my county, it'll make it that much easier to keep an eye on you."

"That's enough, Johnny." Martino turned back to Howard Falcon. "Like I was saying, nice try counselor, but no dice."

"Then I'll file a motion with the court to have the charges dropped. I just wanted to give you the chance to do it yourself rather than having to be told to by the judge."

Martino chuckled. "Well, don't bust your butt getting that all typed up, counselor. Judge Hayes took off this morning a day early for his vacation, and he'll be gone for two weeks while he's fishing for white marlin. The docket's been cleared until he gets back. The judge that's filling in part-time until then is only hearing arraignments and emergencies. Your client's already been arraigned, and this is no emergency. So, you'll just have to wait for a while to hear "no" again."

Howard stood up, our cue to leave this little kangaroo court. Lonnano smirked at me as we left. I'm well on my way to hating that man.

BACK AT *LADY DAWN*, I told Dawn everything that had been said at the meeting. She was as angry as me. "So, now I guess they expect us to go do their job for them? Unreal!"

Rikki said, "If we don't, this will still go to trial, or at least head that way. But with what we already have, there's more than enough evidence to raise reasonable doubt with a jury and get an acquittal."

Falcon replied, "I agree, but you saw Martino. This is his biggest case ever, with his most well-known victim and defendant. It's a small county and they don't even pay to have a full-time judge fill in during Hayes' vacation. So, there's no way Martino will agree to drop the charges until after the election. It's completely political, and good for a lot of free campaign publicity for him. Especially if it looks like he's standing up against what the public sees as a very rich and violent man. And Lonnano sure acts like he has it in for Casey.

"I think Martino may be hoping that we can ultimately prove our theory, especially if that happens after the election. That would get him off the hook, and hopefully serve up another defendant for him to prosecute. Trust me, there's no way he'll let this go all the way to trial though, even if we don't find who's behind this. Whether he wants to publicly admit it or not, he knows his chances of winning are now slim to none. But he won't have the sheriff look into our scenario because I could bring that up in court, making them look like they now doubt that you did it. I don't have to prove that you didn't do it, Casey, I just have to raise reasonable doubt that you might not have."

"No, you do! We have to figure out and prove who framed me. I've lost too much credibility as it is, and even then I won't get it all back. An acquittal won't do it, I need complete vindication with the charges against me dropped, and new ones filed against whoever did this. Reasonable doubt doesn't cut it," I said.

Rikki said, "The key to that is the property and this mysterious buyer who is supposed to be doing some deal in New Jersey. Everything leads back to there."

I nodded, "I think their attorney was caught off guard when the council pressed him to know who his client is beyond just the corporation name. That may have been a mistake on his part. What if he was letting on where the people behind the company are really from, not just where they have another project. They worked hard to make their 'shell company' look Virginian, and to hide who owns it. Too hard. I think their lawyer may have tipped their hand a bit early, or maybe they weren't planning on divulging that at all."

"If that development company is behind all this, they know where to hire leg breakers, hookers, and murderers. And they're smart enough to set you up and take you out of the picture. These guys are pros, Case. Chances are they've done something like this before," Rikki said.

"I'm going to start digging to see if there are any developers in New Jersey who are either based there or that have done work there that are known or suspected of similar crimes. If there are, we can start looking to see if there's any link between them and Cape Charles. I'll also check out that lawyer and firm with my federal friends. If these faceless developers are behind this, chances are their lawyer might be just as slimy. I'll find out what I can." This was right up Rikki's alley. With that, she and Falcon headed back to their offices.

9

NEW DIGS

Bim was staring at the door after Rik and Falcon left, so I told Dawn that I was going to take him for a walk and clear my head a bit. She replied that she was going over to the office building and start getting our new offices set up for the two of us there.

On my way down the dock with Bim, we ran into Murph. "I was just coming to see you, Case. How'd your meeting go?"

I brought him up to speed on what happened as we walked toward the woods beyond the north boundary of the Mallard Cove property. Relating it as one long story allowed me to look at it as a whole, rather than focusing on the bits and pieces as we all had when they trickled in. The only thing that made sense to me right now was the rail yard property was at the center of it all. But why?

We reached a seldom-used trail in the woods just beyond our property line and followed Bimini east as he wandered along a pair of old tire ruts. Walking with my canine pal and my old human friend in the edge of the woods was taking away some of the angst I had been feeling about my current situation. Bimini kept looking back frequently as if to make sure we were still following his lead. I love being able to let him roam without a leash, but not nearly as much as he does.

He stopped and waited for Murph and me to catch up. As we reached him I noticed that from here we could see into the marina property, and also see where that property stopped. East of the in-and-out boat storage barn was a thickly wooded area about thirty yards wide that paralleled the marina's eastern property line on the neighboring property.

We walked beyond those trees to where a marsh grass plain opened up to the right, maybe a hundred yards long and fifty yards wide. Just east of that was the remains of what appeared to be an abandoned boat basin. It had been partially bulkheaded in spots with what were now rotting wooden planks. A crumbling boathouse was in the far left corner of the basin and looked like it hadn't been inhabited in my lifetime. That it had withstood all the storms during this time without any maintenance was a testament to the building practices and materials from "back in the day."

"Wow, Case, I never knew this was here," Murph said.

"I didn't either. I guess it's naturally camouflaged from the Virginia Inside Passage channel. I don't know how many times we've passed right by here when we were going back and forth to Carlton's boatyard. Of course that being there didn't help." I pointed to a derelict wooden freighter that had sunk across the entrance, totally blocking it from shore to shore, probably a hundred feet or more in length. It's not that uncommon to find old, abandoned wrecks along uninhabited shoreline. The boat had to be a century old or more, quite possibly a relic from the steam-power age. But there was no telling exactly how long it had been here; it had probably gotten tossed in its current location by a storm. It was laying over on its side with one rail completely underwater. The part of it that was above the water had plants and grasses growing along its open seams in both its hull and deck.

"From out in the channel it would've looked like an old marsh pond instead of a cove. We wouldn't have been able to see this was a cut back into here," Murph surmised.

Bimini looked up at me curiously, and I pointed around the north side of the basin, "Keep going, Bim." He didn't need any more encouragement and headed off in that direction, occasionally pausing to mark his new territory. We circled around the edge and over to the boathouse. I could only imagine what kinds of cool watercraft had been housed in there, again "back in the day."

I was expecting the area beyond the boathouse on the eastern side of the basin to be marsh and muck. But I was surprised to find that it was firm ground and slightly more elevated than the side closest to *Mallard Cove*.

"Uh, oh," Murph said.

"What?" I asked as I looked around my feet, alarmed. I was halfway expecting to see a snake. But when I looked back up at him, he was grinning.

"I know that look, Case. You get it every time you get interested in a property."

"No, I don't!"

"Riiight. And we've known and worked with each other for what, seventeen years?"

I ignored that. "I just find it interesting that we never knew this was over here, that we always thought of it as just a marsh."

He grinned. "Annnd..."

"What?"

"Now you can see this as something, Case, I *know* you. I've seen you look at buildings and properties that others passed by, and you ended up making hundreds of thousands if not millions on each of them down in south Florida. All after you got this same exact look. Kari gets it too, which is freaky sometimes."

I grunted, "Last time I checked, you were doing quite well as a result of each of us getting 'that look.' So what if I do see something in this place? Something it could be. Maybe even something for all of us. But first, I need to run it past Dawn before I say anything more."

"Okay, I won't say anything until after that." Murph paused, obviously considering something before continuing. "I went looking for you to find out how the meeting went, but to also tell you something."

"And?"

He shook his head. "Oh, no. You're holding out on me, so now I'm returning the favor."

We stared at each other like a pair of old mules on a narrow footpath, neither willing to back up. Finally, I sighed and said, "I've been thinking about what you said yesterday, and you're right. Even if I get exonerated, I can't go back to *Bayside*. There will always be the murmurs behind my back, and the gossips that will keep my innocence in doubt. That'll cost us some business, no matter what, but it'll be less if I'm not there. Cindy can handle it all. I talked with Dawn last night she said that it was like living in a fishbowl, and she's right.

"You were also right about what *Bayside's* crowd is becoming. I'm not as comfortable there as I originally was, and now I'll never have that level of comfort there ever again. *Mallard Cove* is more my style, but there are drawbacks here, too. Like not being able to fit on the private dock with you guys, meaning it could end up being even more of a fishbowl for us. And not having C3 right next door is a big negative. I really love and appreciate that place."

Murph looked across the water, around the field, then back at me. "You're thinking of making this into your own private marina?"

I nodded. "Not in a commercial sense, but yes. I've been thinking of it that way for the last minute and a half since I've never seen it before right now. Lots of 'ifs' though. *If* it's for sale, *if* it's big enough, and *if* we can still deal with the county now after this mess. And the biggest 'if' of them all: *if* I don't go to prison."

"We're not going to let that happen, Case."

"Hope not, Murph. Now, what was it you wanted to tell me?"

He grinned. "I'm taking Lindsay up to dinner at Bayside tonight. Best table at the restaurant, dressed up nice, fine dinner, then I'm going to get that ring on her finger if I have to sit on her to do it."

Murph has a checkered past with women, just ask Dawn about that. But Lindsay has been patient with him, living together for two years, hoping that they might end up getting married at some point. A few months ago she finally ran out of patience and optimism, and they hit a real rough patch because of it. It didn't help that another woman started hitting on him during the couple of days they briefly split. After they made up, he proposed. She said maybe later. It drove him crazy. Since then he's proposed on two other occasions that I know of, all with the same answer.

"Good luck, pal, Lindsay is a great woman, and probably the only one in the world who would be willing to put up with your butt, long-term. I hope this works tonight."

"You and me both, brother, you and me both."

We turned and started making our way back to the office, with Bim now reluctantly taking the lead once again, sad that his outdoor adventure was almost over even though he now had almost nothing left in his bladder to be able to keep marking new territory. Murph and I were silent for the most part on the walk back, both having quite a bit still on our minds.

I SAT in the conference room where my laptop screen was wirelessly replicated on the large flat panel on the wall. I had found the plat for that property online and put it up on a split-screen with an aerial view of the property next to it.

"There you are! I've been looking for you." Dawn walked in then stared at the screen. "What's this?"

"Come sit down and close the door, we need to talk."

Dawn looked concerned as she took a seat.

"Nothing to worry about, Dawn. I'm just trying to add to the list of possibilities I was talking about last night."

She scowled. "As long as one of those isn't you getting locked up."

"Hey, we have the best people trying to make sure I don't. Meanwhile, I'm working on identifying options for when I'm cleared."

Her face softened. "Good. So, what is this?"

"I've been thinking..."

"Oh, no! Nothing good ever comes of that," she joked.

"Seriously, this is about what you said last night, us living in a fishbowl, and you're right. Remember when Sandy Morgan came to Bayside, he complained about the same thing when people started boarding his boat uninvited, wanting books signed or autographs."

Sanford "Sandy" Morgan is a best-selling author who lives aboard his fifty-five-foot trawler along with his niece, Micah Monroe. She and Jeff, the captain of *Predator*, are an "item." Sandy also owns an outfitters shop in the Florida Keys. He and Micah spend their winters there, then migrate back up here in early spring. Sandy taught her the writer's craft, and she's now become successful in her own right.

"Yes, but we fixed that by moving him over to the private dock."

I nodded. "Right, but we don't have that option for us here, and we don't have C3 nice and handy anymore, either. Two points against staying here."

"But it sounds like you've ruled out going back to *Bayside*."

"It's still an option Dawn, just not my favorite. I'm trying to gather as many possibilities as I can, so we can make the best choice."

"And this swamp," she pointed at the wall, "is one?"

"Look closer," I said. I blew up the section with the basin and the boathouse.

"Okaaay? Where is this?"

"About a thousand feet from here, adjoining *Mallard Cove's* eastern property line." I could see the wheels start turning in her head.

"It's big. Is it deep?"

"It appears to be deep enough, but we can always dredge it if we need to. And it's big enough for our two boats plus a few more." I zoomed out to show the overall property, "And there's also room for a copy of C3, and plenty of room for Bim to run."

She raised an eyebrow. "Might be enough room for a couple of houseboats and a couple other boats."

"I thought that too. So, is this an option?"

"I'd say this is a good option, if we can get it for the right price."

"I don't think it would be a good idea for me to go asking around after all the publicity. I'm thinking having Kari do it would be better."

Dawn nodded. "Agreed. Besides, I'd like to hear what she thinks of the idea."

. . .

Two hours later we had a verbal contract on the property. The owner was in a retirement home, with his son handling his finances. He had almost been ready to list the property and was pleased to be able to avoid having to pay a broker's fee. It was his truck's ruts that Murph and I saw, but he hadn't been out to the property in years prior to that.

Speaking of Murph, he and Lindsay were ecstatic over the idea of all of us having a small private compound, as were Kari and Marlin, and all were up for the idea of moving next door. Being able to park right behind their boats without having to dash a couple hundred yards in the rain from their cars was a huge factor. But so was not having to wade through all the tourists on the charter dock, which was between the parking lot and their dock. It also put all our boats closer to our offices, another plus in inclement weather. Now, all I have to do is find out who framed me, then I can close on this land and get started cleaning, renovating, and building.

Roy Roberts pushed his work cart along the dock at the Cape Charles Town Docks. His business was in-water hull cleaning, and today he was hitting six boats in Cape Charles. This next one was a full-keeled thirty-seven-foot sailboat named *Fruitcakes*. He thought, if only he had a dime for every boat in a marina he'd seen named for a Jimmy Buffett song, he'd never have to scrub another bottom.

After setting up his small sandwich board with "Caution: Diver Below!" on the dock, he climbed down into the water on a ladder in the empty slip next to the sailboat. He donned his scuba tank that was hanging from a line and his weight belt which also was tethered with the tools of his trade, a couple of scrapers and brushes.

As he was about to swim over to the boat, something caught his eye in the murky water of the empty slip. He swam to the bottom, about twelve feet below the surface, where he found an electronic box. Judging by its condition, it hadn't been in the water long. People throwing their junk in the water was one of his biggest pet peeves, especially putting old metal junk in boat slips. This can react with the dissimilar metal parts on boats, and the electrolysis that's generated eats away at shafts, rudders, fasteners, or the sacrificial zinc anodes that protect them.

Before he got started on the sailboat, he brought the box to the surface and put it on the dock next to his sign. Then he dove again and got to work. Forty-five-minutes later he returned to the surface, only to find Tim, the dockmaster, standing with Bill Withers at the base of the empty slip.

Tim asked, "Did you find this, Roy?"

"Yeah, it was on the bottom of this slip, why?"

Withers said, "Because it was stolen out of my restaurant two nights ago, and it may show who did it if the cops can still pull anything off the drives."

Just then Lonnano pulled up and got out of his car. After asking Roy a few questions, he put the recorder in his trunk and drove off, but not before warning all three men not to say a word about what they found, saying that it could compromise an ongoing investigation. He would warn the techs at the lab to keep their damn mouths shut, too. There was no rush for them to get to this since he was sure it was only going to show what he already believed to be fact. That it was that damned developer who killed Shalloway and faked being drugged. He wanted to make sure there would be no leaks to any civilians this time, he was going to be the only one to get a copy of whatever might be retrieved from the drive. Shaw and his bunch weren't going to show him up again, or twist the facts to try and get the charges dropped. This case was going to court or else.

10

THE PLAN

Lindsay loved the *Bayside Dining Room* at the resort's hotel, it was the most elegant dining spot on ESVA. Large windows faced the marina and the bay, the wait staff all wearing tuxedo shirts and black vests, with the Maître d' in a full tuxedo. There were elegant linen tablecloths, along with freshly cut flowers and crystal stemware on each table. The place looks every bit as expensive as it is, and the food is as fantastic as the setting.

Lindsay figured this was Murph's "Hail Mary" play to get her to accept his proposal. Ironically, she'd have gladly accepted at almost any point during the two years before their short breakup, but after that she'd been too angry to accept. She wanted it to mean something other than being a peace offering from him and not part of the memory of the rough patch. Lindsay figured that the time was finally right, and she decided to accept tonight if he asked. Then they'd have this romantic dinner as the memory of the moment.

They'd no sooner been seated at one of the two best tables up against windows facing out onto the bay before they spotted a helicopter approaching out over the water. It passed low over the marina, banking toward the helipad in *Bayside Estates*. The pad had been Casey's idea, making the trip from DC easier for Eric Clarke and some of the other wealthier guests who had access to helicopters. Murph didn't recognize the chopper, it wasn't Eric's Sikorsky, but instead a smaller Bell 407 that appeared to be brand new. Casey had mentioned there were a couple of different helicopters that had been in and out lately. Two minutes after this one landed they heard it take off again, but it must've been headed east since they didn't see it come by.

The maître d' casually mentioned that one of the people who had just flown in was the Chief of Virginia's Matunkey Indian Tribe. Then he handed Lindsay and Murph their menus and took their drink order. The drinks quickly arrived, and they took their time deciding what to eat while slowly enjoying their libations. They just ordered when Cindy escorted two men up to the maître d', handing them off to him after telling the larger man that should he need anything, to ask for her. They were then seated at the table behind Lindsay, also next to the large window. Both men looked to be in their early fifties, one was of average height with very tan skin and a long black braided ponytail, dressed in a simple navy off-the-rack suit. The other man was short, slightly portly, and balding with a gray combover. He was dressed in what no doubt was a very expensive and tailored charcoal suit with light-colored stripes that made the outfit look like something out of the nineteen-twenties.

As Cindy turned to leave she spotted Murph and Lindsay. She approached their table, smiling.

"Big night out, kids?"

"Nothing out of the ordinary," Murph said.

Lindsay chuckled. "Don't let him kid you Cindy, any night I get him to eat inside a restaurant in a coat and tie and in long pants during warm weather is special."

Cindy spotted a small square bulge the size of a ring box in Murph's coat pocket, and put two and two together. She knew what had been going on between them. "Well, you guys enjoy your dinner, and let's catch up soon." She winked at Lindsay as she turned and left.

Two minutes later their server approached with a champagne

bucket and two flutes. She set the glasses on the table and removed the bottle from the bucket for Murph to see the label.

"Uh, I didn't order any champagne." Murph looked confused.

Their server replied, "It's compliments of Ms. Crenshaw."

"Aw, that's so sweet! Please thank her for us if she's still around," Lindsay said.

The server smiled, "She's always around."

AT THE OTHER TABLE, Joey Newell and Chief Joway Collins had heard the exchange between the three. One of the acoustical quirks of this dining room was that when people sat at certain angles at these two particular tables, their voices bounced off the glass window and they didn't need to strain to overhear each other.

The maître d' approached Joey's table with a bottle of wine, turning it so that Joey could read the label. "Compliments of the management. Ms. Crenshaw hopes that you two gentlemen will enjoy your stay with us."

Joey said, "Whatta you guys give out wine like this alla time?" He motioned to Murph and Lindsay.

"No sir. That couple are personal friends of Ms. Crenshaw, but we do usually send a bottle to guests who occupy our finest suites upon their arrival. In your case, she wanted to send it to your table since you came in to dine first."

Joey read the label, "Hey, that's good stuff!"

The maître d' smiled. "Yes sir. Shall I open it?"

"Well, I ain't gonna just look at it." He looked across the table at his dinner companion. "See why I brought you here, Chief? This is what we gotta do at our new place. It's this kinda stuff we need for the level of players we wanna attract. Our place'll be just as fancy so we get high-income people in that don't figure on gamblin' but most'll end up getting' lured in anyways. We're gonna compete with this place, too."

· · ·

JOEY ENDED up ordering another bottle in addition to cocktails, and by the end of dinner, both he and his companion's voice levels had gone up by several decibels. Murph and Lindsay finished their entrees about the same time and were now sharing a slice of twelve-layer Smith Island cake, a Chesapeake Bay delicacy. Joey and the Chief had decided to drink their desserts, and soon their voices got even louder. They were now beginning a business conversation.

"Joey, I'm worried. I heard there was serious competition for our project. If we don't end up with the land..."

"Chief, like I told ya, that's my end. Just like the management of the place'll be my end, too. All you gotta do is play landlord. Thirty-five stories high worth of landlord." Joey looked around, lowering his voice to a level he thought could only be heard by the two of them, not realizing they were still being heard by Murph and Lindsay as well. "Trust me, I took care of the competition. Nobody in Cape Charles'll be goin' after that rail yard but you an' me now. I took care a that damn double dippin' mayor, an' made it look like our competition did it. Anybody else comes outta the woodwork, and they'll end up just like the mayor."

Murph almost choked on a bite of cake. Lindsay's eyes went wide as she stared across the table at him. He made a very subtle patting motion with his hand down next to the plate, urging her to be cool. But both of them were now hanging on every word being spoken by the two men.

"I don't know, I don't want any part of that..." The Chief sounded worried.

"Hey! Who was it tracked you down and showed you dat you was the only hunnerd-percent Matunkey left? And what that meant to you? All you'se gotta do is sign onna dotted line, then start cashin' the checks. You like flyin' around in choppers an' private jets, right? Then trust me, I got this. Just thank your ancestor's spirit, or whatever it is ya do, for him signin' that Treaty of 1677, an' for him sendin' me ta you."

The Chief said angrily, "It was a 'her,' the Queen of the Matunkey. And you mean the Treaty of Middle Plantation, where they forced us to give up our land if we wanted to be able to live in safety. Just like paying protection to you and your pals today, only this was the English!"

"Whoa, Chief, it waddn't me, okay! I'm the guy who's gonna help ya make money because of it, remember? You'll get yer land back an' then some. Youse just gotta trust me on this. So, take a chill pill and relax. And speakin' of relaxin', I got a surprise for you." He pointed out the window where the lights of his helicopter were becoming brighter in the night's darkness as it was approaching on a return trip.

"My associate is bringin' in some, uh, special entertainment for tonight. One of our side businesses is runnin' real high-class broads. Gonna fit in great with the casino. Wait'll you meet these two tonight. Youse can't even tell they're pros. An' don't worry, like everything on this trip, that tab's on me."

The Chief was faced away from Murph and Lindsay, and if he reacted to the news, they couldn't hear or see it. But five minutes later two stunning women walked in and over to Joey's table. He introduced both to the Chief, then suggested they walk over next door to the *Beach Café & Bar* for drinks and dancing. As the four left, Murph noticed a large man had been loitering outside the entrance to the dining room, he had apparently arrived with the women. After Joey nodded to him, he fell in step behind the four. Murph knew a body-guard when he saw one. So, whoever this "Joey" guy is, he takes precautions.

Murph quickly paid their bill, forgetting at least temporarily about the original purpose for their night out. So did Lindsay, as their mission for the rest of the night now shifted to helping Casey. They found the maître d' and asked if he had seen Cindy.

"I think she may have left for the evening. Was there a problem with your dinner?" He looked concerned.

Lindsay smiled, reassuring him. "No, it was perfect. We just wanted to thank her for the champagne, that was so sweet of her."

He also smiled in return and nodded, "She's quite a wonderful person."

"We'll catch up with her later," Lindsay said. She and Murph headed for the front door of the hotel and she dialed Cindy's number.

"Hi Lindsay, are you calling with some news?" Cindy teased her, then became serious when she heard Lindsay's tone.

"Murph and I need to talk with you and Rik. Where are you guys?"

"We're both on the boat. What's wrong, Linds?"

"Not on the phone. We'll be there in two minutes."

THE FOUR SAT in the salon of *Hibiscus*, as Lindsay and Murph related what they had overheard. Cindy looked stunned, but Rikki never missed a beat.

"Cin, what do you know about that guy?"

"His name is Joey Newell, and he's from Foal Neck, New Jersey. Booked two of our best suites for the next two weeks. Flew in on a chartered helicopter, and brought the Chief of the Matunkey Indian tribe with him as his guest."

Rikki looked at Murph and Lindsay, "If what you heard was right, this guy is a stone-cold killer. Wait here a minute."

Rikki walked out onto *Hibiscus'* back deck, returning five minutes later after making a call. She looked concerned. "According to my source with the Feds, Foal Neck is a mob stronghold, a neutral territory for all the families that have country homes there. Joey Newell isn't a 'made guy,' but a wannabe.

"They heard he did a favor for the boss of the mid-Atlantic. A big favor. His reward was being handed a project in the ESVA territory, and enough money to charter helicopters and rent suites. They know there isn't a lot going on here right now because of the low population. But the boss figured with the scheduled expansion of the Bridge-Tunnel to four lanes, and with more people moving away from the cities and to the coasts, this area will be growing rapidly and he wants a foothold when it does. Rather than send one of his more important guys, he sent Joey as kind of a test for him.

"Joey's known as an aggressive guy who wants to move up, and he must've come up with this plan on his own to impress the boss. A high-rise casino and high-class hookers sound right up his alley as a base starting point. But I don't understand how he expects to be allowed to put in a casino in Cape Charles. No way the Commonwealth would ever permit that."

Lindsay said, "It has to have something to do with that treaty they were toasting, and that chief being the last one-hundred-percent Matunkey Indian."

Because of Cindy's background in the Virginia hospitality industry, she was familiar with casino regulations. "The indigenous tribes of the Commonwealth have the right to open gaming operations on reservation lands, but only there. And neither Cape Charles nor any of ESVA is part of a reservation."

"We'll have to do more digging and find out what the connection is. Meanwhile, you two need to get back to *Mallard Cove* and brief Casey and Dawn. If we thought this thing was bad enough before, it's really bad now. They need to watch their step and make sure that Newell doesn't find out that we're wise to what he's up to. We have to figure out a way to clear Casey's name without that happening," Rikki said. "They'll need to keep a very low profile in the meantime."

THE FOUR OF us met in the salon of *Lady Dawn*.

"Organized crime? In Cape Charles?" Dawn was astonished.

I said, "It's the closest town to the bridge-tunnel, and most likely one to expand since they already have that mindset. Most of the rest of ESVA wants things left alone. And a casino? There's no way the Virginia General Assembly will go for that, much less the people of Cape Charles."

"He seems pretty confident, Case," Murph said.

"He may be, but why?"

Murph replied, "Rikki thinks there's a connection between that treaty and the casino."

"Can I borrow that?" Lindsay pointed to Dawn's tablet on the coffee table.

"Be my guest." Dawn handed it over and watched as Lindsay started digging on the internet. Over the next ten minutes her facial expressions showed that she wasn't finding what she was looking for. I mixed drinks for everyone, but Lindsay was on the hunt and set hers down absentmindedly without even taking a sip.

Finally, she must've had some luck as she started smiling. When she looked up she said, "You know the problem with most of these websites? They give a condensed version of things, and they get to choose what they include. Fourteen tribes signed that treaty. It was all about a consolidation of most of the indigenous tribes of Virginia for their own protection. They were under attack from various colonial militias who wanted to grab their land. So, about a dozen tribes merged into two larger groups, living on a handful of reservations, and were granted protection by the King of England over the colonial groups after swearing allegiance to the king. Nothing about ESVA or casinos though."

"Sure sounds like organized crime to me. 'Join up and live where we say, or you're on your own,'" remarked Dawn.

"Pretty much, Dawn. But one tribe held things up for quite a while until they got a special deal. Any guesses which one?"

I said, "The Matunkey?"

"Give that man one of Baloney's cigars! Any guesses where they originally lived?"

Dawn said, "ESVA?"

"Exactly! The queen of the tribe argued that they could defend themselves here, and she didn't want to give up their land and move west. But the Governor saw the potential for another massacre of a tribe and wanted to be able to deliver a complete agreement to the king of England. So, he was willing to make a deal."

Lindsay looked at the three of us with a smug grin. "This chick was nobody's fool. She knew that once things were settled down by this treaty, in another generation or so the memory of the conflict would have faded. So she had an amendment added to the treaty specifically between the Matunkey and the king of England. It says that after fifty years, any land formerly held by the Matunkey prior to the treaty which might be legally reacquired by them can be subject to the laws and rules of all other Indian lands in Virginia. She didn't want her tribe confined to a reservation with combined tribes, she wanted to retain their identity."

Lindsay held up the tablet showing that separate page. "Because it only applied to one of the smaller of the fourteen tribes, it became a separate page and one of those footnotes that almost got lost in history. Luckily this historical society managed to preserve that last page, or it would've been lost forever. Later the newly formed United States of America accepted the treaties as they were, and they stand in effect still today."

It hit me like a ton of bricks, "This gives that chief the right to essentially turn the rail yards and any other property on ESVA into a new reservation. Then he can do anything he wants. He's not limited to building four stories there like Cape Charles allows, he can go thirty-five stories like that Joey guy said. Or even taller. No architectural review, no inspections, no nothing."

"Right, Case, but it's not him, it's Joey Newell. The chief is just a tool he's using to allow him to do this. Joey called him the landlord," Lindsay reminded us. "Somehow he figured out this deal, and then found the chief."

"And Joey is a pawn for one of the heads of organized crime in New Jersey. So, by pulling this off, creating the only high-rise money-laundering hotel and casino on the Eastern Shore, it would be a huge feather in his cap and probably give him a leg up in the organization. And he's not about to let anyone or anything stand in his way," I said. "Well, there are two things I want to do now. The first is clear my name, and the second is stop Joey Newell."

11

THE BOATHOUSE

M *onday morning in Cape Charles...*

As VICE-MAYOR, Larry Markham had taken over as mayor when Shalloway died, and he was now meeting with Joey's lawyer at the attorney's request.

"Mayor, I appreciate the council's having extended the timeframe for applications for my client. With all that has gone on, it's in everyone's best interest to move forward swiftly so that there can be some positive news from Cape Charles, then we can all get past the negative news cycle." He placed a set of rolled-up renderings on Markham's desk.

"Here is our plan for the rail yard parcel. You can see that it's very similar to the plans from M&S Partners, as we both seem to have the same type of vision for the property. If you wouldn't mind passing along the copies to the other council members, then you can go ahead and award us the property at this next meeting, and we won't have to wait the additional two weeks for another meeting."

Markham looked taken aback. "Mighty sure of yourself, aren't you? What makes you think that you'll get the property and not M&S?"

The lawyer looked shocked, "You aren't seriously still considering M&S after the head of the company murdered your mayor, are you?"

"You know that Mr. Shaw has not been convicted of Mayor Shalloway's murder, and if we dropped them from consideration because he's been charged, that could leave the town wide open to litigation. So, the answer to your question is yes, we are still strongly considering them. Shaw's partners are a very impressive group, and even if he were to be convicted, I'm sure that they would have him step down. In fact, we would probably stipulate that in any agreement.

"Their group has a lot more going for them right now, not the least of which is that we know the identity of all the partners, and the fact that all but one live here on ESVA. So, you're going to have to have a much more impressive proposal than just a look-alike of their plan if you expect to be awarded the property. And if this is all you have today, then we're done here."

The attorney glared at him then stood and left without a word. Markham remained seated. The attorney was ticked off at having been dismissed by this hick-town politician, but he was even more scared about having to convey this news to Joey. Word was that his mentor back in New Jersey was furious over the way Joey had handled both the mayor and Shaw, calling it sloppy. If he didn't close on the property and clean up this deal, well, the lawyer wouldn't want to be him.

"Hey, Case." Rikki came into the conference room at the office in *Mallard Cove* and took a seat next to me.

"Hey, Rik. Should I read something into the fact that you drove here instead of calling?" I hadn't known she was coming by.

"I was on my way to the Shop at Norfolk, but I got a call from my friend at the FBI." The Shop is where the operations group and the majority of the employees of ESVA Security work in total secrecy. "He said that they were now quietly taking over the Shalloway murder investigation after finding out about what Murph and Lindsay overheard. Apparently, Lonnano and Martino are stonewalling, trying to keep it in their local jurisdiction even though they know about the linkage to the Delaware murders. The feds are less than pleased about that. You are really on Lonnano's bad side, and he still wants to pin it all on you."

"Doesn't surprise me, Rik. He's an obstinate SOB."

"The feds will be by this morning to chat with you. My friend said they weren't all that impressed with what Lonnano has done so far, and they're retracing all his steps."

Again, I wasn't surprised. "Glad to tell them all I know."

She passed her tablet to me, with a man's face on the screen. "Newell. Just so you know what he looks like."

"Yeah, I can't believe he's up enjoying *Bayside*, and yet he's the reason I had to leave."

Rik replied, "If we kick him out of there, we'll tip our hand that we know what's going on. Better to have him there where we can keep an eye on him. It takes a major set of cojones for him to stay there, and we want him as overconfident as possible right now. I'll send this pic to Dawn since Murph, Linds and Cindy already know what he looks like."

She looked over at the plat and sketches I had out on the table, showing the layout of my proposed docks. "Another marina, Case?"

"Small one, just next door. Figuring on building a private compound down here."

I caught her off-guard with that. "What, and move down here full time? You don't need to do that, we're going to get these charges dropped and then you can come back home." She looked concerned and started to sound defensive. "As board members, we had an obligation to do what was best for the *Bayside* investment at the time, Case, but we weren't suggesting that you leave permanently."

"I know, Rik, and I'm not blaming you guys, it was ultimately my decision to leave. But it wouldn't be the same if I went back after all this. Plus, this is a better place to have *Predator*. Take a left, and we're in the Atlantic for offshore and near-shore fishing. A right puts us in the Chesapeake or at the bridge islands. More options just makes more sense. Jeff's bringing her down this morning. Another plus is having Dawn's and my offices here, it puts us in the middle between the Lynnhaven project and *Bayside*."

"I'll miss you guys being on the dock. Cindy will too." The concern in her voice was now mixed with sadness.

I nodded. "Thanks. But you know what? Having Cindy take over all the *Bayside* operations was a great thing to come out of this, and that wouldn't have happened for a while if we had stayed there. I'd never want to let go, and she wouldn't have been able to reach her full potential until I did. Remember that old saying, 'Lead, follow, or get the hell out of the way.'

"Not too long ago you were pushing me to take more time off and fish, remember? And now I've realized that we've got the right people in the right places, so I think I will slow down a bit and do just that. Maybe this thing is a reminder to me to let everybody do as much as they are comfortable with. And I'm comfortable with Cindy handling all of *Bayside*."

Rikki said, "That's what she's loved so much about working with you, Case, is you let her do everything she feels capable of doing. I've learned a lot by watching you, and it's helped me with my own associates in my business. People like being given all the responsibility they can handle.

"On the other hand, you've got people like Lonnano, who try to take more responsibility than they should. Most likely the sheriff and the Commonwealth Attorney aren't strong enough to reel this jerk back in. He's got Martino wrapped around his little finger."

I agreed. "Yeah, I don't get that, but I've seen a lot of Lonnanos in my life. Bullies that move from the schoolyard into positions with a little bit of power, and they find a way to leverage it against others. It wouldn't surprise me if he wasn't trying to set himself up to be sheriff in a few years. Dropping charges against me isn't going to get that done for him."

Rik nodded, "I agree, but that's his problem. At least, I want to make sure that it's his problem."

"WHATTA YA MEAN they're still in it? That shoulda taken 'em out!" Joey and his lawyer were meeting in his suite at *Bayside*.

"The new mayor said that because Shaw hasn't been convicted of killing Shalloway, they can't drop him from the list or the town could get sued. It's what I told you I was afraid might happen." The lawyer realized he shouldn't have added the last sentence as it was coming out of his mouth, but by then it was too late.

Joey exploded. "Did you just tell me 'I toldya so?' You know what happened to the last guy that had the balls to say something like that to me? He don't got 'em no more! Get the hell outta here, I'll take care a this myself."

After the lawyer left the room Joey motioned to his bodyguard to come over, he had been hovering behind the lawyer during the conversation. "This guy Shaw. If somethin' happened to him now, maybe an accident, his partners ain't gonna want ta keep goin' with tryin' to get that property, you know what I mean? An, everybody in Cape Charles will remember him as the guy who took out the mayor. So, you know what needs to happen."

"I got it, Joey."

"Me an' the chief are gonna get seen around this place the rest of the day."

The bodyguard nodded before leaving the room. He knew he had until the end of the day to take care of the problem, while Joey and the chief were alibied up.

AFTER RIK LEFT to catch up with her team and to try to find more proof linking Joey Newell to the murder, I wanted to take my time and see as much of that property next door as I could. I went back to the boat and put on hiking boots, and Bim looked up expectantly as I got ready to leave.

"Sorry, partner. I'm going to get into some gnarly areas, and I don't feel like having to wash a bunch of mud off you when I get back. Stay here, and we'll go for a fun walk later." Bimini glared at me before he went over and curled up in his bed in the salon with his favorite cow bone, holding a one dog pity party.

I suppose that I should've paid more attention to my surroundings when I crossed through the marina parking lot on my way to the woods, especially since Bim wasn't with me. While the rental car wouldn't have rated a second glance since it was tourist season, the fact that the guy inside it was wearing a windbreaker on such a calm, hot, steamy day sure should have.

I followed the same route that Bim, Murph, and I had before. This time though, I was more focused on the actual basin at the end, trying to discern the depth from the angle of the shoreline. That turned out to be an exercise in futility as the native grasses and reeds grew down to the dark water's edge, all the way around the basin.

"Don't do anything stupid." The voice came from behind me, and I turned to find a hulk of a guy with a large framed semi-automatic pistol with an equally large silencer on the end of the barrel. "Get your hands up where I can see 'em."

I slowly raised my hands up to shoulder level. Hulk Junior here was good, staying just far enough back to avoid getting jumped, but still close enough so he wouldn't miss if I ran. Normally I carry a concealed firearm, but since I hadn't planned on leaving *Mallard Cove*, I hadn't felt the need. That, and the fact I wasn't sure exactly what the terms of my release were and if I was still allowed to carry my pistol. I hadn't wanted to take any chances with Lonnano dying for an excuse to lock me back up, so it was back on the table next to my bed. Even if I'd had a gun, my chances of getting to it before being ventilated by this guy were probably next to none.

"All right, now head over to that boathouse." He emphasized the direction by waving the barrel of the gun.

I started walking slowly, stalling for time so I could think. We were too far from the marina for anyone to hear if I yelled for help, and that silencer would deaden any gunshot; it would never be heard beyond the property line. Maybe if we were going inside the boathouse there might be something I could use as a weapon, and give me a chance to fight back. Neither Murph nor I had gone inside that day we were over here, and I hadn't been back since. I have a strict rule about not "romancing" a property that I'm interested in. If you are seen making too many visits before you get it under contract, any leverage you might have to negotiate the price goes out the window.

It looked like we were going inside, as Hulk said, "Open it."

The door had a broken hasp hanging with an old rusty padlock still attached, it hadn't been much in the way of protection from a break-in long ago. I tried the doorknob and it turned. The rusted hinges resisted a little before the door swung open, revealing a crumbling "u" shaped dock inside surrounding the water. The basin end of the building was open; the hinges of its doors having failed long ago, letting them fall into the water.

"Keep goin'." Hulk had a definite Jersey accent, and there was little doubt as to who he was working for. Joey Newell wouldn't get his hands dirty himself like this.

I stepped gingerly onto the dock planks, half expecting them to give way, but they didn't. A disappointing look around the mostly dark and vacant interior failed to turn up anything that could be used for a weapon.

"Keep goin, over by the edge."

I moved in another ten feet before I stopped. A metallic snapping sound had me turning back to the Hulkster, who was now brandishing a collapsible metal baton that he had extended. I glanced at the water and then back at the man, who was moving closer, the baton raising above his head.

"I know you're thinkin' about jumpin' in the water. If you do, I'll just hafta shoot you, and I'll make sure that it'll be in a real painful place so you'll bleed out slow. This way, one crack on the head and it's lights out, then you drown while you're knocked out, all peaceful like."

I said, "Oh, gee, thanks for being so considerate."

He laughed. "It ain't that, it's because Joey wants it to look like an accident. You get found full of lead, and things get more... complicated when they find ya."

"You mean Joey Newell. And I guess the bullets in those three bodies in Delaware would match up with any others fired from that gun so, yeah, it would get complicated."

Hulk laughed. "Nah, only an idiot woulda kept that gun. I got rid of it the first bridge I crossed comin' back. This is a new one, and I really don't want ta hafta toss it, I kinda like it. An' yeah, Joey Newell sends his regards, just like he did for those three." He flashed a crocodile smile as he raised the baton higher.

"Freeze, FBI! Drop the weapons!" An all-business female voice called from the doorway.

I hit the deck because I figured the Hulk wasn't in the mood to comply. I was right, he started shooting as he spun toward the doorway. His silenced shots went wide and he never had a chance to zero in on his target. Hers didn't, as she hit him twice in his chest before the Hulkster dropped over the side of the dock, his body slowly sinking below the surface.

"Shaw, are you all right?"

"I'm... good," I said after all my extremities had reported in. "Who are you, and thank you, by the way."

She walked in through the doorway, replacing her pistol in her belt holster. "FBI Special Agent Stephanie Baker, Mr. Shaw, and you're welcome. That was a close one for both of us."

"I'll say. I'm lucky you came along when you did."

"I was actually here to follow up on your statement to Detective Lonnano when I spotted Sal Ricci following you across the parking lot at the marina."

"Sal Ricci? That's the guy's name?" I asked.

"Joey Newell's right-hand man, bodyguard and problem solver, but with what I overheard between the two of you, now his chief problem maker. Nice, you getting all that out of him."

I shook my head, "I wasn't trying to get him to confess, I was just stalling for time. Hoping to figure my way out of that, which wasn't happening until you came along. I had no idea you were there."

"Well, that was lucky for both of us. You're still alive, and now we have enough to charge Joey for all those murders, too. C'mon out of here, I need to call the evidence team since this is now a crime scene."

When we walked out into the daylight I saw that she was a very attractive brunette about my age. She had a confident air about her as she called it in, not seeming to be a bit nervous, despite having just shot and killed a suspect while taking fire herself. Talk about one cool character.

As for me, I was now starting to shake. Honestly, from the time we entered the boathouse I thought it was over, and that I was going to die. There was no way out for me that I could see. Now since I lived through that, several things had come more into focus. There are things I wanted to do, needed to do, and that I was going to make happen.

12

NEW BEGININGS

Within an hour the boathouse area was crawling with FBI evidence specialists, divers, and supervisors. Sal's car was towed from the marina parking lot, and I was now back aboard *Lady Dawn* with Dawn. Word had spread fast around the marina about all the cars with government license plates that had been rolling in. Murph, Linds, Marlin, and Kari all stopped by the boat for a few minutes, wanting to know what happened and find out if I was okay. I had stopped shaking by the time they all left. Well, almost.

Rikki called, already having all the details and adding a few of her own. Joey Newell had been hauled out of *Bayside* in handcuffs and was being charged with numerous crimes, including conspiracy to commit murder. My murder. That just sounds creepy saying it, especially since it came so close to happening.

Rik also told me that jerk Lonnano had been hiding the fact that he had the security video recorder from the *Shack*. The crime lab had able to recover most of the stored video, including the part about me being dragged to the car. It also clearly showed me being driven away and back again by that couple who murdered Shalloway and then met by Sal Ricci and another woman.

I was now officially cleared of any charges, and Martino and

Lonnano's crazy theory was dead. But I was still pissed. They had known I was innocent, and this charade had been all about politics; they weren't going to release this "new" information until after the election. Now I planned on making a big campaign donation to Martino's opponent, whoever he or she might be.

"Jeeze, I just heard about alla this on the VHF, Case. You okay?" A clearly shaken Baloney had barged in through the dockside door without knocking.

"I'm good, Baloney. Looks like this thing is almost over. I just have to get this damn anklet off and I'll be happy."

"Oh, that's good, I was worried. Hey, can I grab a..."

I couldn't help but smile. "Help yourself to a beer, Bill." Baloney does have his priorities in order.

There was a knock at the same dockside salon door, and Dawn answered it. It came from one of the last people I expected to see at *Mallard Cove*. "I hear there was all kinds of crazy happenings around here today. Hey, do you have a beer, Casey? I'm fresh out."

"Help yourself, Sandy, you know where they live. What the hell are you doing here, by the way?" Baloney gave Sandy Morgan a concerned glare as he grabbed a cold Red Stripe from the bar refrigerator.

"You left, and suddenly it got real boring around *Bayside*. Plus, with Jeff bringing *Predator* down here, Micah was going to be driving back and forth to see him anyway, so I decided to come see what all the fuss was about this place. I like it, so you can consider me as being moved down here as well. I was starting to run out of decent characters and plots up at *Bayside* anyway. Now with you and Dawn gone, only the hoity-toity crowd was left, and they're no fun." He suddenly noticed Baloney glaring at him, or more specifically, his beer. "And what the hell's your problem, shorty?"

When Bill's ever-present unlit cigar starts moving back and forth between the two corners of his mouth, the best move is to get a libation, sit back and watch the show that's about to start.

"Shorty? Who the hell are you, besides a friggin' beer mooch?"

Baloney gets really protective about "his" beer, even when it belongs to someone else.

"Somebody you don't want to piss off, that's who. Hey Casey, where'd you get this guy? Wherever it was, I hope they have a return policy." He turned back to Bill, "Just who might *you* be? You look like the captain from that movie, *Mr. Roberts*."

"I am *Captain* Bill Cooper. You know, from *Tuna Hunters*." Baloney's chest puffed out.

"Big commercial boat name for a little fella's boat."

In reality, Sandy was only five-feet-nine-inches tall, but that still made him four inches taller than Bill.

"It's not a boat, it's a top-rated TV show I'm in, you moron!"

"Oh. Excuse the hell out of me for never having heard of it, Gilligan." Turning back to me again, "As I was saying, I was running out of material up there, but if you've got more characters around like Gilligan here, this place could be a gold mine of inspiration."

You're probably thinking this is Sandy's way of getting my mind off my earlier excitement. You'd be wrong. It's just Sandy being Sandy.

Bill piped back up, "So, you'se didn't tell me who the hell you are."

"You're right, I didn't. And what are you, fresh off the Cape May ferry with that accent? You need to come with your own Jersey to English dictionary."

As I said a while back, Bill thinks he lost his Jersey accent long ago and gets ruffled when anyone brings it up, so the cigar is moving back and forth at warp speed now. But Bill still loves and will defend everything that has to do with his native state, especially his two boats that were built in New Jersey.

"Casey, who is this guy?" Baloney more demanded than asked me.

"Baloney, meet Sanford Morgan, best-selling author of dozens of books about coastal adventures."

Sandy replied, "Waterfront escapism."

Baloney said, "Never heard of you or that escape stuff."

Sandy snorted, "There's a big surprise. I doubt you ever read anything past the Dick and Jane books in elementary school. Baloney, eh? That name sounds like it fits you really well, Gilligan." He took a long draw off his beer and returned Bill's glare.

"Yeah, well, I can think of a few names for you too, fella."

Before Baloney could bestow a nickname on Sandy, there was another knock at the door. Our steward Andrea answered it, and it turned out to be a stern-faced sheriff and a sour-faced detective Lonnano. The sheriff approached me, and I stood to meet him, shaking his outstretched hand.

"Mr. Shaw, on behalf of our department, I apologize for the way your case was handled. This isn't the way that our deputies, and especially our detectives, are supposed to conduct themselves." He paused to give Lonnano a sideways glare, "Regardless of their political ambitions."

I could see that Lonnano wanted to be anywhere but here. The sheriff apparently now knew all about his political plans, and how he and Martino had been working together to keep the charges against me active until after the election.

The sheriff pointed toward my ankle, "Get that thing off of him."

Lonnano bent down with a tool that unlocked the electronic anklet, releasing the strap that held it in place. As he stood back up, the look he shot me wasn't one of contrition, as much as of contempt. This guy might have the sheriff fooled, but I could tell he wasn't the least bit sorry for having done what he had, he was just sorry he and Martino had gotten caught. I wasn't about to let this go, either.

"So, no apology from you eh, Lonnano?" I asked, not really expecting one.

"Okay, I'm sorry. But I was just doing my job, and everything pointed at you."

"No, it didn't, and you've damn well known that for a while. I've been a supporter of law enforcement my whole life. I respect the hell out of the ninety-nine point nine percent of the officers that do the job because they love it, even though they might hate the politics that comes with it. You, on the other hand, are the worst kind of unrepentant ass that puts the politics above the job, and ahead of the people you are supposed to protect and serve.

"Do you have any idea how much permanent damage you've done to my reputation, and my company? Do you? Well, you might very soon if I file a lawsuit against you personally over it. Now get the hell off my boat, and out of our marina."

At the mention of a lawsuit, I saw him lose a shade or two of color in his face. He left without another word. The sheriff looked worried, still standing there.

"Mr. Shaw, it wasn't the intention of our office to continue to charge an innocent man."

"That may be, sheriff, but it happened. And you and your department are responsible for the conduct of your deputies. My reputation has suffered harm through no fault of my own, and there's nothing I can do to completely restore it. I don't even feel comfortable returning to *Bayside* since my being there now might cost us business. And my partners and I may miss out on our opportunity to acquire and develop the Cape Charles property because of this, too. That's an awful lot of damage, all because of the sloppy work by your detective and the ambitions of both him and the commonwealth's attorney."

I could see the sheriff was a quick thinker, and I knew he was well connected, politically. He looked like he was weighing some options right now. I was about to find out if he could act as fast as he thought, and how many "markers" he might have out there to collect on.

"Mr. Shaw, could we meet in private tomorrow morning say, around nine? Maybe there's a way we can make amends for what has happened."

As angry as I am, I can't help but like the sheriff. Yes, he's ultimately responsible for the conduct of those under him in his department. But right now I'm curious to see what he's planning to do to mitigate the damage that's been caused.

"All right, sheriff. Give me a call in the morning, and we can meet back here."

"Thank you."

After he had left, Sandy said, "You're letting him off the hook real easy."

"Oh, I haven't let him off the hook yet. I have an idea where he's headed. But he's about to find out that I want more than he thinks." I smiled.

"I seen that smile before, an' I wouldn't want to be that guy when he comes back," Baloney said.

"Bill, you know I'm a reasonable guy. But I'm on some pretty firm ground, and the local 'powers that be' would be dumb not to deal with me."

"I'm thinkin' so, too." He headed for the bar 'fridge and another beer, glaring at Sandy as he did.

WHEN WE MET AGAIN the next morning on *Lady Dawn,* I had Dawn with me. The sheriff had Larry Markham plus the head of the Northampton Board of Supervisors, Bill Smathers.

Larry Markham said, "We appreciate the opportunity to talk this over all off the record, Casey. I want you to know how I'm sorry I am about everything that happened, especially since it all started when you and I had dinner."

Larry's a good guy. He knows this isn't the best way to open a negotiation, by apologizing up front, but I could see that he meant what he said, and I appreciated his candor.

"So am I, Larry, though it had to have started way before that. And I'm guessing that you've probably never seen the inside of the sheriff's jail. Well, I wouldn't recommend it." The sheriff grimaced when I said that, but I wanted to set the tone on my side. I had been wronged, and I wanted the three of them to keep that in mind.

"I can imagine." He paused a beat then said, "This is a huge mess, Casey. You and your group aren't the only ones who have been hurt by this, though you've for sure borne the brunt of it. But Cape Charles has taken a hit to our reputation, too. You know how the negative publicity of a lawsuit would just draw it out and make it that much worse. What could begin to repair it for all of us is if your group is still willing to move forward with your plans for the rail yards. It would send out a very positive message."

I nodded slightly as if thinking it over as I turned next to the county supervisor. "I had to move out of my resort or risk losing business simply because I was there. People think I'm a murderer. That was my home, and now I've lost my ability to stay there unless I'm willing to cost my shareholders and myself some of our business, which of course I'm not." The supervisor squirmed slightly. "So now I've been forced to move down here, and I've lost the life and the comforts that I built and enjoyed at *Bayside*. I want that back, or something approaching it."

Quickly he replied, "How could we help with that?" He knew I'd win any lawsuit, so I knew he'd like to avoid one.

I leaned back on my sofa. "I've figured out a way that won't cost the three of you a dime, and we all end up happy."

He looked both hopeful and skeptical. "I'd love to hear it."

"Since going back to *Bayside* is no longer an option, Dawn and I just bought the property next door to this one. Our objective is to build a setup similar to what we had there. We want to put in private docks, a pool, and a small residential building. But I also want to add a helicopter pad and a seaplane ramp, neither of which are allowed by the current zoning. In fact, I don't want any problems from the building department or any county interference on what I want to build there."

"Done, I'll get you the zoning variances for those and whatever else you want." Smathers was relieved.

Then I said, "Good. And yes, Larry, we do still want the rail yard property."

"We'll handle that at the next meeting, Casey. Done deal."

I had one last item. "Sheriff, that just leaves your department. What's going to happen to Lonnano?"

"He's suspended without pay for two weeks and received a written reprimand in his file."

I nodded. "He'll have it in for me when he gets back."

"He might, but everyone in my department is well aware of what occurred, and you won't have any problems from anyone. If you do, please call me directly. And I understand the commonwealth's attorney is also getting a reprimand from Richmond for his part in things."

Howard Falcon knew where the political bodies were buried in Richmond, and he'd been making a few calls, reminding folks of that. Martino's political future now looked bleak.

THE THREE OF them were a heck of a lot more relieved when they left than they had been when they arrived. And while I wouldn't want to have to go through what I had ever again, it's funny the way things have a way of working themselves out when you let them. Knowing that I had no limit to whatever we want to build next door was almost worth the price I had to pay to get it.

"Since when do we own a helicopter and a seaplane?" Dawn asked.

I grinned, "You never know what's in the future. And chances are I'd never have another opportunity like this one to get whatever zoning variances we want. This way if we ever do decide to get either of those, we already have the pad and the ramp in place. Eric will get some use out of the helo pad in the meantime, I'm sure."

"Everything else will be a copy of what we had at Bayside?"

I replied, "No, there are a few changes I have in mind, and I want your input too. Now I want to get the deal closed and get started. The sooner we get it all built and the boats moved over, the better. Then I can put this all behind me. Behind us. I want to get back to being able to relax, and forget this ever happened."

"THE FEDS GOT HIM? You gotta be kiddin' me! Of all the dumbass moves, this one's the worst. First he blows the casino deal and gets caught doin' it. Now he can't even clean things up right." Joey's mentor was furious. "Leaves me a mess I gotta take care of."

His lieutenant was trying not to show that his hands were shaking, but Paulie Attanasio's temper was legendary. And murderous.

"So, here's the deal. We let this calm down a couple of weeks. Joey ain't goin' nowhere, and he ain't gonna say nothin'. Then we quietly clean things up. What a dumbass move by Joey, tryin' to frame one of the richest guys on ESVA when there was other, less messy ways ta get the job done. Now we're gonna do it my way. Get word to him that he's gotta take the fall, I don't want any of that crap blowin' back on me. Whatta they got him on, conspiracy? If he takes a plea, he'll only get five, maybe seven years. It'd be good for him, toughen him up a little.

"Now we gotta make sure nobody is gonna steal our idea. If I was that chief, I'd be tryin' to sell it. We do all the homework on this thing an now somebody else can walk in and take it? I don't think so. Nobody's gonna do that ta me."

13

LOOSE ENDS

T*wo weeks later...*

THE SITE WAS in a state of absolute pandemonium. A hog-wire fence was going in around the twenty-one-acre property's perimeter, a gravel drive had replaced the muddy truck ruts that led in from the road, floating docks that had been built on land were now being swung into place by a crane. Normally it would've taken half a year or longer to get the state and federal permits for the docks, but since the freighter blocked the entrance it's technically a pond. At least that's my story, and I'm sticking to it. Taking the freighter out and opening that entrance will happen later this week after all the docks are in place, and when we're ready to dredge parts of the basin a little deeper.

"Not letting the grass grow under your feet, as usual." Murph's voice made me jump, I'd been so intent on watching the work I hadn't noticed him walk up. He handed me a "to-go" cup of coffee from the *Mallard Cove Restaurant.*

"Thanks for this, and no, I'm not." I laughed. He knew I was never happier than when construction was going on, except maybe when I was fishing or flying. We stood at the edge of the water, watching as another long section of dock was "flown" into place by the crane.

"So, I took Linds over to *Arthur's Bistro* in VA Beach last night."

I haven't been there but I knew it was expensive and elegant. "Swanky."

"Yeah. After what happened at *Bayside*, I wanted a different setting."

"Un huh. And?"

"I finally got that ring on her finger." He grinned, almost sheepishly.

"Hey! Congratulations! We all need to celebrate tonight. Let's cook out on *Lady Dawn*."

"I don't know, Case, you think that will go over well with Dawn? I mean, with our history and everything."

"You know she's mellowed. And she is going to want to celebrate with Linds no matter what, so yes I know it'll be fine."

I texted Dawn, who had just heard the news from Lindsay. She loved the cookout idea and suggested adding Marlin and Kari. I left it to her to invite them. I no sooner finished my text when my phone rang.

"Mr. Shaw? Special Agent Stephanie Baker."

"Hi, agent Baker. What can I do for you?"

"I need to let you know that the body of the Matunkey tribe's chief was discovered a short time ago. He was executed, shot twice in the back of the head."

I had started to relax again over these last two weeks, but that all went out the window in a split second. "You think it was Joey Newell?"

"He's still in jail, so obviously it couldn't have been him personally. But doing things personally hasn't been his way the past few years. I can tell you this much, the chief managed to live his whole life in peace until he got tied up with Joey."

"So why kill him?"

She said, "If I had to guess, I'd say ego. Since Joey was never going to be able to build the casino concept he came up with, killing the chief made sure that nobody else would either. That and the fact that the chief was a loose end. He was back on the reservation before we got a chance to talk to him, and then he refused to cooperate or answer any questions."

"And there are two other loose ends that are still keeping Joey in jail right now." I subconsciously felt for the Glock 19 I had in my small-of-the-back holster. I had gotten back into the habit of carrying it with me everywhere after my run-in with Sal Ricci.

"We can't say for certain that it was Joey, but keep your eyes open just in case."

I said, "Trust me on that. You do the same."

She replied, "Oh, I will."

I hung up as Murph looked worriedly at me. "Who?"

"The Matunkey chief. May have been Joey, but maybe not."

"I wouldn't put money against him, would you?"

I shook my head, "Not likely."

"They think he's coming after you?"

"That's unknown. Killing the chief would have been to block anybody else from being able to do what Joey had planned to."

Murph said, "If this guy was willing to kill again just over that, and you and that agent are the only things standing between him and a conviction, why don't they put you in protective custody until the trial?"

"They can't be sure Joey had him killed. And Joey hasn't threatened either of us, at least not directly. Besides, there's no way I'd agree to going anywhere."

"At least call Rikki and bring her up to date."

Murph had no more gotten that sentence out when my phone rang again. It was Rikki. I said, "I take it you've heard."

"Yes. And I have Dave headed your way. Where exactly are you?"

"At the little cove." I thought about telling her to turn Dave around, that I could take care of myself, but she knows that. Plus, I know all the members of her team are all trained in a lot of areas including surveillance, and that might come in handy if Joey comes after me. Having an extra set of eyes around, especially professional eyes, wouldn't be such a bad thing.

"I'm glad you aren't going to fight me on this, Case. The more I dig into it, the less I like it. Joey may be directing a few things around ESVA, but he isn't the one who's really pulling the strings."

"Then who is?"

"Paulie Attanasio. Big guy out of Foal Neck, New Jersey. Runs most of the mid-Atlantic."

I asked, "By 'runs' you mean…"

"I mean he owns the mob concession on everything illegal. That kind of 'runs.' Apparently Joey had curried some favor with him by coming up with the casino idea. Instead of expanding into new territory and having to fight to do it, Paulie saw an opportunity to create new business opportunities within a growing area inside his existing territory. This project was going to punch Joey's ticket to the big time."

"Since that's gone away, the only thing he's got left to look forward to is getting out of jail. And Agent Baker and I are standing right in between him and the front door."

"Like I said, Dave is on the way."

~

"What's the news?" Joey asked his defense attorney, Randy Peterson.

"It's not good, Joey. With the testimony of that FBI agent as well as this Casey Shaw character, their case is pretty much airtight. I'm doing my best, but Sal really blew it for you."

"Yeah. That wasn't like him, he hadta figure there was no way Shaw was ever gonna say anything ta anybody ever again."

"If only. And there's another wrinkle in all this now. Somebody took out your Indian pal last night."

The shocked look that Joey now gave Peterson told him everything he needed to know; Joey hadn't done it. He watched his client lean back in the steel chair, thinking rapidly before he leaned forward over the desk.

Peterson said, "And there's more. Paulie says to make this up to him you gotta take a plea. I think I can get you six or seven years, and you'll be out in four or five."

Joey's eyes widened farther, then narrowed. "But I wanna beat this."

"Joey, Paulie was serious. We need to work on getting you a plea bargain deal. I can let them know we're open to it."

"Gimme your notepad and a pen." Joey scribbled a note then slid the folded paper across the desk. "I need you ta drop this off in Virginia Beach, at the Golden Gal strip club wit a guy named 'Jimmy the Eye.'"

Peterson didn't say a word, he just took the folded note and buried it in a stack of paper in his briefcase on the desk. Most lawyers know better than to do what Joey was asking him to, but most lawyers aren't on retainer by people on the fringe of the mob. And it would be Joey's funeral, not his. He hoped.

"Hey Dave, good to see you again. Kind of." I grinned, greeting him as an old acquaintance. Dave had been part of a security team that had guarded Marlin after he had run into a bit of trouble in the past, and at one point he had flown down to Florida with us on my plane. He's big, quiet, and smart. He also blends in well in long khakis and an untucked button-down vented fishing shirt that hides his semi-auto pistol.

"Hi, Casey. Good to see you, except for the circumstances. I read the brief about what happened to you, and Rikki filled me in on the latest."

Like I said, Dave's smart. "Yeah. You probably know more about what's going on than me. What's your take on it?"

"I think it's a good thing that I'm here."

Dave doesn't mince words. I nodded, "In that case, I'm glad you are too."

We hung around the job-site until lunch, then walked back to the boat for a bite. I saw Dave constantly scanning the area as we walked. While it was the *Cove's* busy season, it was midweek. If people were here on vacation, chances are they were at the hotel pool, the beach, or out fishing, or on one of the *Pelican Fleet's* charter or rental boats.

Unlike *Bayside*, which is a much pricier marina with more expensive boats and professional crews, there were only a few full-time crews on the private sportfishing boats here. Many of the boats are older and cost only a fraction of what a newer one does, and are "owner/operator" setups. Most are maintained by their owners, though a lot of the grunt work is farmed out to kids and independent contractors. There are boatmen that are always around, doing the work and trying to pick up business during the week. We see most of the boat owners showing up by midday on Fridays. They usually stay aboard for the weekend then head back to their businesses in VA Beach, Richmond, or Charlottesville on Monday mornings.

We went aboard *Lady Dawn,* and I showed Dave our onboard security setup. Cameras covered the exterior decks and one was trained down the dock. There were numerous screens located on each interior deck and in our stateroom. Motion sensors can also be set to cover the exterior approaches, and Dave seemed satisfied with our system. We went up to the highest deck, the flybridge & entertainment deck where he did a threat assessment. He decided the upper gunwales provided enough cover to deem this area safe for me to use.

"Just keep the drapes closed in the salon and your stateroom at night. No sense broadcasting who is moving around, and giving someone a shot at you from long range. But they don't have a shooting angle here if you stay away from the open aft part of the deck."

I replied, "I'll do all that." Like I said, I'm glad he's here.

∾

LEAVING the small field office at the end of the day, Special Agent Baker was looking forward to a nice dinner date with someone she had just begun seeing. The anticipation of the evening had thrown her just slightly off her game, so she completely missed the threat just as I had with Sal. Fumbling with and then dropping her keys as she was about to open her car door was what saved her life. The driver's window of her car exploded into a shower of tiny bits of glass that rained down on her back as she bent over to pick up the key ring.

Hearing the shot as the glass simultaneously dumped on her, she stayed down between her car and the one next to it. Silently drawing her Glock 17M from her holster, she lay down flat alongside the glass bits and peered under the other car in the direction of the shot. A pair of sneakers came sprinting across the open middle lane of the parking garage, stopping three cars away from her own. They began slowly and stealthily making their way toward her car, as their owner used the three vehicles between them for cover.

When the sneakers stopped on the other side of the car next to her, Special Agent Baker drew a bead on the shooter's left ankle and fired. Her bonded jacket nine-millimeter hollow-point bullet brought the shooter down to her level, his ankle now an orthopedic surgeon's nightmare. When he refused to toss his pistol away at her command and instead tried targeting her, she shot him again. This bullet went in his side, ripping through lungs and arteries, ensuring that an orthopedic surgeon wouldn't be needed.

She stood up cautiously, looking for any accomplices of the shooter. Seeing none, she checked him to make sure he wouldn't be getting up again. She saw two fellow agents entering the garage, guns drawn. With a huge sigh, she was sure of two things: her date was going to be canceled, and now with two bodies to her credit in as many weeks, the paperwork was going to be huge.

"JOEY DID *WHAT*?" Paulie was furious after hearing about the attempt on Special Agent Baker. "Nobody goes after a Fed! That's suicide, it'll bring them down on all a us. We don't need them digging around, and stirrin' up more trouble, it's bad for business. This has gotta stop. Now we gotta give 'em something so's they can close the case, if you catch my drift." He stared at his lieutenant.

"They just moved him to the Federal lockup in Richmond."

Joey smiled. "That should make things that much easier. I bet you can find somebody in there who owes us a favor."

"I got it, boss. I'll take care of it. No more trouble."

"Yeah, that's the last of the loose ends."

DAVE LEFT JUST BEFORE DARK, as our guests were arriving. The six of us went up to the top deck where the crew had set out hors d'oeuvres on the bar and prepped the gas grill station for me to cook steaks. Yes, we have a chef aboard who would have been happy to cook the meal, and a steward who would have gladly bartended, but then this celebration wouldn't have the casual "feel" that we wanted it to. This was Dawn's and my gift to our friends, and we wanted it to be personal, so we split the duties.

We had just finished dinner when Rikki called with the news about the attack on Agent Baker. I instinctively glanced over at the video monitor behind the bar, which currently was displaying the feeds from four of the security cameras. Dawn had seen me tense up and followed my gaze as I scanned the dock feed. Fortunately, there was no movement showing. I thanked Rik and hung up.

"What is it Casey," Dawn asked.

I shook my head, not wanting to worry our guests, but they were all now looking at me.

"Case?" Murph said.

I sighed, and related what Rikki had told me, including that they weren't certain that this was connected with Joey's case.

"You've got to figure it is. Just to be on the safe side," Murph replied.

"I suppose so." Though I wasn't a hundred percent convinced.

Probably only ninety-nine percent. But it put a damper on the rest of the evening, which then ended earlier than I had wanted it to. I had planned for cigars and brandy to cap off the celebration, but now the time just didn't seem right.

Twenty minutes later Dawn and I accompanied our guests out to the gangway at the exterior deck beside the salon as we said good-night. In the low light, the red laser dot showed up brightly on my chest as Murph instinctively reacted by tackling me, dropping me below the gunwale and down to the teak deck, and yelling for everyone else to get down. Two shots rang out from a couple of boats over.

After what felt like an eternity but in reality was probably only thirty seconds, Dave's voice came from down the dock, "We're secure, Casey, but all of you need to get back inside the boat."

We did what Dave said, though it was killing me not to go racing down the dock to check on him. Within a couple of minutes, we heard the first of what would be almost a dozen sirens. Half an hour later Dave walked in, accompanied by Special Agent Baker.

Dave asked, "Everyone okay?"

I answered, "We are, but how about you?"

"I'm good, his shot went wide. But I was on target."

Baker said, "Meaning that he disabled the shooter, but still left enough meat intact for us to be able to question him after he gets out of surgery. I wasn't that lucky with mine this afternoon. We should be able to get some answers out of this guy though in a few hours."

Dawn said, "I thought you went home, Dave?"

"I did, but after Special Agent Baker was attacked, Rikki had a hunch and called me back in. And I remembered seeing a guy this morning on that old fifty-three foot Hatteras with the brokerage sign on it. The guy was waxing the aft cabin bulkhead in the hot morning sun. Had he waited an hour, the sun would've been on the bow, instead of baking the fishing cockpit. Any professional boatman would have known to do that. Plus, the paint on that old boat is shot, and it's up for sale. Most brokerage boats the owners won't spend a dime on, other than washing them down occasionally. Why would somebody be paying to have that old paint waxed? That's when it hit me, this just gave him an excuse to be able to watch everybody coming and going on the dock, and to determine a shooting lane from there to here.

"Sure enough, when I pulled up I used a night scope from my car and I could just make out that guy, crouched below the cockpit gunwale, waiting for you to say goodnight to your guests. I snuck up behind the dock box behind the next boat and waited for him to make a move. I blinded him with a tactical LED flashlight so he'll be seeing spots for days. He tried to shoot me, but I took out his shooting shoulder. His tennis-playing days are over."

Talk about two pros - Dave and Baker were both calm, cool, and collected, despite both being involved in shootouts today. As for me, I was still shaken after having had yet another brush with the grim reaper. But I had enough of my wits about me to be able to give a statement.

Rik arrived with a replacement for Dave, to let him have some "downtime" after the shooting. "Case, we're going to keep someone with you twenty-four hours a day until Joey's trial is over. Fortunately, we had Dave today, because even with Murph shoving you down, if that guy had started shooting through the fiberglass gunwale, things could have ended much differently."

"I'm not going to argue, that's for sure. Thanks, Rik. And thank you again, Dave. I owe you."

"Just glad you're okay, Casey, and that things ended well for our side," Dave said.

Our side. I had been thinking in terms of just me, but it was true that I owed my safety tonight to a team effort. A damn good one, too. I came within seconds of... Suddenly I realized I needed to talk with Dawn after everyone leaves. It was half an hour later when it was down to just us two. I made us each a vodka, and we sat together on one of the couches.

"I want to move things up," I said.

"What are you talking about?"

"The wedding. I don't want to wait until next year. This was my second brush with death in as many weeks, and not many people get second chances."

"You're just having a knee-jerk reaction to all of this."

"Damn right I am, Dawn, and I'm glad I still can. I want to finish the new docks, get moved in next door, and then get married this fall. If you do."

"I said I'd wait as long as it takes, but yes I'd love to get married this fall. We can have the wedding and a small reception up at my folk's in Easton, then the following weekend have a big bash here at our new home with all our friends. If you can get it all finished by then." She gave me her best challenging look.

"Trust me, I'll get it done on time. I'm glad you wanted to have it here, rather than at *Bayside*."

"No, *Bayside* is just about business from now on. The little cove is all about being home."

That's part of why I love this woman so much, we think alike about most everything. And as much as I enjoyed being there before all this started, she's right, *Bayside* is just an investment now. Our little cove *is* home.

14

WINTER'S HERE

E*arly the next morning...*

MY CALLER ID said it was Rikki. Since it was barely light out, I knew whatever this was about was big. I was having my first cup of coffee at the crew's table in the galley. "Hey, Rik."

"Hey, Case. Joey Newell's dead. They found him in his cell this morning, he hung himself during the night, supposedly."

Suddenly I felt like I was on my third cup of expresso. "What's that mean?"

"It means pal, that you're no longer a threat to Paulie Attanasio. But I think he saw Joey as one. With him now out of the way, Paulie shouldn't give you another thought, if he ever did in the first place. I'm pretty sure this was all Joey's doing."

I haven't been this relieved since that day they dropped the charges against me. Still, I was cautious. "Are you sure?"

"As sure as I can be, though I'd probably keep my eyes open and I wouldn't stop carrying a firearm, just in case."

"Sounds like a good plan, I usually do both anyway. I can't tell you how great it feels to get my life back."

"I bet. Maybe now we can get around to doing some fishing."

"We need to plan on that, Rik. You know, like we discussed, there are a few things I've been meaning to do that I'm going to scratch off my list, and I think I'll start today."

"You're a good man, Case. And after the month you've had, I think that might not be a bad plan."

Dawn came into the galley after I hung up with Rikki, and I brought her up to date as she grabbed a coffee and sat next to me at the crew's booth. Then she gave me her challenging look again. "Then are we still on the same timeline for...things?"

"Oh, yeah, I can have the new docks finished in a couple of weeks, and we'll be rocking on C2 shortly."

"You know that was only part of what I was asking, and what's a C2?"

I smiled, "Yes I know, I was just seeing what you'd say. Also yes, I still want to get married this fall. And C2 is short for the *Cove Club*, the name for our new hangout and home."

"I like the way you think. To both of those."

WE HAD a nice relaxed and leisurely breakfast together, the first I'd had since we arrived at *Mallard Cove*. Finally, I was ready to get out and get busy.

"I have one more thing to scratch off my list this week."

Dawn asked, "Which is?"

"A surprise. Been meaning to do it for over a year, but never got around to it. I'm not putting anything else off, from now on. You'll see."

I kissed her now furrowed brow then slid out of the booth, making myself a "to go" cup of coffee before heading down the dock. I stopped at the Hatteras that was involved in the shooting last night and saw there were several wrappers from the paramedic's supplies that had been used on the shooter, as well as a large area of blood on the deck. Since the shooter had been after me, I felt kind of responsible, and called the dockmaster and asked him to hire one of the dock kids to clean it up and charge it to me.

I moved one boat over, to another brokerage boat. This one was a production center console outboard, about twenty-five feet. I was about to go aboard for a closer look when I heard a familiar voice.

"Ya know, every time I get around you bombs go off or bullets start flyin'. I hear Murph saved yer butt last night."

"Hey, Baloney. Yeah, I owe him one. Dave, too. Both those guys were looking out for me."

His cigar bounced up and down in agreement with what I'd said. "What're you up to here?"

"I've been meaning to get an outboard that I can zip around in and run out in front and do a little fishing by myself."

"An' you're lookin' at one of *these* things?"

"I take it you don't like this brand?"

He looked like he had bitten into a lemon. "Lemme put it this way, if I had a daughter in a whorehouse and a son in one of these, I'd get my son out of it first."

I laughed. "Okay, what's wrong with them?"

The cigar shifted from one side of his mouth to the other before he continued. "They only put about half the fiberglass in it that they shoulda, you can almost read a newspaper through the side. Plus, it's a hard ridin' sumbitch. You put those two things together an' it's a recipe for disaster down the road. When a builder cuts costs startin' at the hull thickness, you don't just walk away from the boat, you better *run!*"

Bill may be a little rough around the edges, but when it comes to boats, I trust his opinion. "Okay, let me hit you with this and see what you think. I want a single-engine outboard center console, about twenty-four or twenty-five feet. I'd like a soft ride, and maybe thirty knots or so at wide-open-throttle. A boat that's easy to single-hand, and has all rounded edges. Any ideas?"

Baloney smiled. "This same broker just brought one in over on the first dock. Twenty-four foot Winter, a custom North Carolina boat. Sounds just like what you're lookin' for, and it's a real looker."

"Eric bought a smaller one of those for his daughter, a great little hull. But I don't want all the teak upkeep that comes with something that fancy."

"Didja miss the part about it bein' custom there, Casey? No two of 'em are the same. This one's a real fisherman's boat, all paint 'cept for the varnished helm pod on the console. That's the only teak in the whole rig. I'll show ya."

Baloney led me over to the first dock where the most beautiful outboard I'd seen in a while lay in its slip. Flared Carolina bow, everything flush-mounted, t-top with outriggers, leaning post, baitwell, and a full transom with a single 300 horsepower engine on a bracket. At first glance this one seemed to check all the boxes for me, plus it was sexy as hell. Bill and I climbed in and looked it over more closely, and it was everything I wanted. I called the broker's cell phone. He gave me an abbreviated spiel, then hit me with the price. And I do mean "hit." Way more than what I had in mind, so I didn't pursue it any farther. I thought it was strange though that the broker gave up so quickly, without trying harder to get an offer out of me though.

I thanked Bill, then headed over to the C2 job-site, disappointed over the Winter. Could I have afforded the asking price? Yes, but just because I *could've* doesn't mean I *should've* jumped on it. If you get a reputation for being a spendthrift, you're screwed. Word gets around fast that you're loose with your money, and pretty soon you won't have any. And it wasn't like there weren't other boats for sale. But I *really* liked that one. And like Bill had said, they were all "one-offs," meaning there wasn't another one exactly like it.

"You don't look happy."

I jumped, as Murph had once again snuck up on me. "Jeeze! Would you quit doing that?"

"What? Saving your life, or bringing you coffee?" He grinned as he passed me another "to-go" cup. "What're you so grumpy about? I thought you'd be happy that you lived to see another day."

"That part, I'm happy about. In fact, I've decided to do a few things I've been putting off." I told him about moving up the wedding, and then the story about the Winter.

"Congrats on the wedding part, but the boat part makes no sense. I know the guy who owns that boat, he's getting divorced and told me he needs to move it fast." He paused a minute then said, "Actually, I know that broker too, Jim Smith, he's a major league slimeball from VA Beach."

I asked, "Think he's trying to stall so he can pick it up for a fire sale price himself?"

"That would be my guess. Let me call the owner."

It turned out that the price I had been quoted was way over what he had agreed to with Smith. Murph told him that I was a qualified buyer with cash in hand, and he said he'd meet us at the boat himself in thirty minutes.

On our way back to the Winter, we ran into Sandy. "Good morning, gents! I heard tell about a bit of excitement after I hit my bunk last night. You all right, Casey?"

"I'm good, Sandy, thanks."

"Yeah, I'm good too, Sandy, thanks for asking," Murph grumped.

"Murph probably saved my life, Sandy." I told him the full story.

"Yep, moving down here was a great choice, plenty to write about. Except for the part about having to wade through the tourists on the charter docks to get to my boat."

Sandy was on the private dock on the far side of the basin, and it gave me an idea. I texted Dawn then said to Sandy, "We're going to try to make a deal on a boat. If I do, we'll go for a sea trial. You want to come along?"

"Probably no story in it, but what the hell, I just sent my latest book off for editing so, sure. I've got time."

THE WINTER'S OWNER, Skip Carson, turned out to be a nice guy in a tough spot. After talking a few minutes we were able to agree on a very reasonable price and took the boat out for a sea trial. She performed perfectly even with four of us aboard and was exactly what I had in mind. As we pulled back into the marina, Murph spotted one very pissed off broker waiting for us at the slip.

"He sure doesn't look happy."

Skip said, "Probably because I called and reamed him out for running off a potential buyer."

Jim Smith came out on the finger pier as we secured the boat. He started yelling at Murph, "What the hell happened to my Hatteras listing? Some kid is over there washing down a ton of blood."

I spoke up, "That's from a guy who tried to kill me last night. He's not doing very well today. And then you tried to screw me this morning. Not a very smart move Smith, making me mad. Just ask anybody."

The broker looked at Murph, who nodded solemnly. "He's my pal, but I don't even want to piss him off like you did this morning. He just got out of jail after he beat that last murder rap."

Smith looked like he was trying to decide if Murph was pulling his chain or not, then decided to ignore him and get back to focusing on what he came here for.

"Okay, whatever. But I'll take it from here, Skip."

This guy is a serious jerk. I said, "No, you won't. I'm not dealing with you, I'm dealing with Skip, you blew your chance."

"Not while I have a brokerage contract with him you won't."

Skip said, "A contract that you breached this morning by trying to run off a qualified buyer."

"Hey! I was just trying to get you top dollar."

I said, "Top dollar was Skip's asking price, not asking plus fifty percent."

"That's up to me as to what I ask."

"No, it isn't," Skip said. "You were trying to run him off and wait until I was in enough of a squeeze that I'd have to sell to you at what you already offered. You're fired."

Murph was amused. "So, you already made an offer on a boat that you're representing? Then you tried to run off a capable buyer with a price well above asking? You're a bigger scumbag that I gave you credit for. You know, if you wad that contract up enough times, you might make it soft enough to use as toilet paper, but that's about all it's good for now."

The guy flared at Murph, "Well, I've got half a dozen brokerage boats in here so you better just butt out, Murphy, unless you want to lose all that dockage."

Murph replied, "*Mallard Cove* doesn't need to be associated with the likes of you." He turned and faced Casey, "Hey Case, you think we should start our own yacht brokerage? With slimeballs like this guy around, we'll clean up by running an honest business. Oh, and you *had* a half dozen brokerage boats in here. But we'll be contacting the owners and telling them you're now banned from *Mallard Cove*, so you can't show their boats here anymore. But we'll offer them a couple months of free dockage if they sign up with our new brokerage."

"You can't do that!"

I said, "I think we just did. Yeah, Murph, I'm in."

"I'll sue you, Murphy! That's restraint of trade or something."

"No, it's really not. But you *are* trespassing now. I meant it, you're banned from here, so get going."

I added, "I'm his partner, and did you miss the part about what happened on the Hatteras? I don't take things to court."

Again he looked like he couldn't decide if I was serious or not, then not so confidently said, "You two haven't heard the last from me!"

Murph replied, "I'm shaking in my dock-siders. Now, get lost!"

As the broker quickly retreated down the dock after giving us all a one-finger salute, Sandy said, "Yep, this was a good move, coming here. I think I just got the opening scene for my next book."

My phone binged, and I smiled at what I read and handed it to Murph who also smiled and nodded. I said, "Sandy, if you'll hang around a little bit while Skip and I complete our transaction, I have something I want to show you."

. . .

AFTER A VERY HAPPY Skip Carson left, check in hand, Dawn joined the three of us over at the *Cove Club*. Sandy was dumbfounded. "I had no idea this was here. I heard the construction noise, but I couldn't see anything. When did you buy this?"

I said, "Last week. We're putting together an even better version of C3 over there, we're cutting through and putting in an electric gate for cars and golf carts to access it behind the in-and-out storage building, and there will be covered carports behind the boats." I started pointing out the slips, "After we take out that freighter, *Lady Dawn* goes over here, then *Predator* next to her. Murph and Linds' house barge, *On Coastal Time*, Marlin & Kari's vintage Chris Craft *Why Knot,* and their house barge *Tied Knot*, their Gold Line outboard *Marlinspike* are all next. My new Winter and everybody's kayaks will be in the boathouse."

Sandy nodded and said sarcastically, "Ah yes, we can't forget the recycled milk-jug fleet." Sandy's not a fan of paddling and kayaks.

Dawn chuckled, "Exactly. And your trawler between the boathouse and *Marlinspike*. If you want that slip. Wait, what new Winter?"

Sandy didn't hesitate. "Heck yes, I'll take it! Covered parking right behind the boat? Privacy to be able to write, yet I can roam around next door for inspiration? Wait, is that Baloney fella going to have a key to the security gate?"

I said, "I'm afraid there's no getting away from Bill anywhere Sandy, but then what would you have to write about if you could? Uh, dear, I forgot to tell you, I bought another boat this morning."

"What kind of Winter?"

After I described the new center console, she got a great grin on her face. "That's perfect for me and the gals, thank you Casey!"

"Wait, what?"

"Nice size for Linds, Kari, and me to go out after work to wet a line, just the three of us."

"Uh, yeah, that's exactly what I had in mind when I picked it out."

Sandy laughed, "Chapter number two! It's a good thing I write fiction."

"You know, in the past, I've had to get divorced in order to lose things like that boat."

Dawn grinned, "Oh, you're not losing it, we'll invite you to go with us every now and then. Let's finish Sandy's tour here, then I want to go see my new boat."

"*Your* boat..."

"Okay, *our* new boat. I've been thinking that we needed one that we could use as a tender for *Lady Dawn*, and I even thought about picking one out."

I said, "Great minds think alike. And right now, I'm thinking you can pay for it!"

"Hah! We can go 'hafizes' if you want."

I rolled my eyes, "So then you'll let me use my own boat. How generous of you." I was kidding, of course. Probably.

"Oh, you can use it on occasion." She smiled again. She was kidding, I think.

DAWN TURNED out to be as taken with the Winter as I was, if not more so. The two of us went out for a quick run, and that was the clincher. There's no ride like that of a fiberglass over cold-molded wood hull, and the design of this one makes it handle like a dream. It's also not as loud as an all-fiberglass hull; the wood tends to dampen a lot of the vibration from the engine and the waves. The full transom deflects what little engine noise comes from the four-stroke outboard, making it easy to talk and be heard at cruising speed. The wind is the biggest noise.

"I love this boat Case, I can't wait to take it out fishing."

"Then get the girls to go this afternoon after work."

"But you haven't even fished it yet. I was just kidding earlier."

Despite her protest, I could see she loved the idea. "Oh, I'll have plenty of time for that. I'm just glad to see you so happy with it, too."

"What's not to love? I mean, *Predator* is fun with a group or fishing a tournament, but this boat's perfect for spur-of-the-moment fishing, or riding up to the *Bluffs*. Buy you lunch at the *Beach Bar*, and we can toss around names?"

"Deal."

I loved watching Dawn run the boat, her long red hair streaming behind her, bright blue eyes scanning the water ahead. She caught me looking at her, a big smile on my face.

"What," she asked.

"Oh, just thinking," I said.

"About?"

"How good you look at the helm." She smiled appreciatively at me until I added, "And how it's going to take an industrial-strength hairbrush to get all the tangles out of your hair!"

She punched my shoulder as I laughed long and hard. It felt good to laugh like that again, it was the first time since I had been arrested. I was glad to put this nightmare behind me and turn a few pages, adding *C2* and the Winter. It was time to put some fun back in life.

15

FOLLOWING THE DREAM

"Jimmy the Eye" Impasato looked grim, sitting in his office at the Golden Gal strip club in VA Beach. It was the top-rated strip club, due mostly to the fact that the girls who performed there were the hottest and the most, well, *accommodating* in town. Because of it, Impasato did well. Quite well in fact, though you'd never know it to look at the place from the outside. The exterior walls were clad in cheap textured plywood, painted in a battleship gray. That paint was now faded and peeling, and the parking lot was in dire need of another layer of asphalt. But no-one comes here for the exterior aesthetics, and Jimmy didn't want to make it look like he had too much cash to throw around. He knew that a lot of guys in his business go to jail thanks to the IRS, not the FBI.

"How bad is my cousin?" He asked his lieutenant, "Tony Pro" Giamatti.

"One to the shoulder. He'll live, but he's gonna do time when he gets out of the hospital. But that ain't all, Jimmy."

"Yeah?"

"Joey's dead."

Jimmy's day just got worse by a factor of ten. Not only had the other shooter he hired gotten capped yesterday going after a Fed, but his cousin had also been wounded trying to take out this Shaw guy. To top it all off, he had pre-paid both of them, fronting the money to Joey until after he got the charges dropped and was released from jail. Now Jimmy was out mid-five figures and sweating whether or not his cousin Bobby would rat him out for a plea deal. Too many trails could lead straight back to him. Once Bobby gets released from the hospital and there aren't any more nurses to look at, Jimmy knew he might get weak. Bobby loves his broads almost as much as Tony Pro, and once the idea of him being locked up for years hits home, well, Jimmy knew it wasn't gonna be good. As the boss, he knew that sometimes you have to make the tough choices.

He rubbed his forehead as he thought, then looked over at Tony and said, "Get Angela in here, I've got a job for her. Then I want you to go find out everything you can about this guy Shaw. I'm out a pile of dough, and I want it back, with interest. I think he's the one who oughta pay.

"Bobby said Shaw lives on a boat over at Mallard Cove on ESVA with some broad and they're both loaded. That's where you should start. But keep it low-key, we don't want to draw any attention. I gotta find out what's the best way to get leverage on him. Bobby said he found his picture on the internet, use your phone and find it."

"WHAT ARE YOU THINKING, CASEY?"

Dawn and I were having lunch at the *Cove Beach Bar*, hoping our beachside table would provide some inspiration for the Winter's name. So far we weren't having any luck. She had suggested naming it after me, since our other boats had either her first name or her old nickname in them but I vetoed that idea, not wanting to name it after either of us.

I said, "I think we need to quit trying so hard. The harder we work at this, the worse the names keep getting. It'll come to us if we just let it."

Looking out over the water between Fisherman and Smith

islands out to the Atlantic beyond, you'd think with this view it would be tough not to get inspired enough to pick a name, but it was.

"Oh, there's a good one," Dawn giggled. A red "go-fast" style boat about thirty-feet-long was slowing as it approached the marina entrance. "*Wet Dream*" was spelled out in huge white cursive letters down the side.

"Uh, I'll pass, seeing as how it's already taken." I rolled my eyes.

The guy running the boat fit the profile of who you'd expect to have a rig like that with that name. Even from a few hundred yards away we could see his dark tan, bleached hair, polo shirt, and aviator sunglasses. A real "sport." Even with it now at idle and us sitting off to the side, we could still hear the unmuffled exhaust rumbling. Everything about the boat screamed "look at me." That's when it hit me.

"How about '*Incognito?*'"

Dawn brightened, "Hmmm, I like it. Not named after either of us and the opposite of a billboard like that 'go fast.' And more in tune with our new lower-key lifestyle at the *Cove Club*. That works, *Incognito* it is."

TEN MINUTES later the guy from the 'go-fast' walked in, and I spotted him right away. Heavy gold chains, gold bracelet, and a big gold watch along with his gym-built muscles made this guy a perfect stereotype to fit the boat. The sunglasses were now hanging from the vee neck of his shirt as he scanned the bar. His eyes seemed to show a faint glimmer of recognition when they met mine, and the hair on the back of my neck stood up. I'd never seen this guy before, at least not that I remembered, but his gaze stayed on me just a bit too long for comfort before he resumed his scan of the bar crowd.

Over at *Bayside* I was used to being recognized by customers I had never met before, mostly because of that *Chesapeake Bay Today* article. A lot of our clientele over there read that magazine, but this guy didn't look like one of their subscribers. Heck, this troglodyte didn't even look like he could read. On a normal summer's day, the *Beach*

Bar gets its share of hotshots like him. But this hadn't been a normal week or even month for me. All kinds of alarm bells were going off in my head.

He went over and took a seat at the bar where he had a nice view of the water. And our table. It was the perfect vantage point where he could watch us from without being too obvious. Except that I was now more vigilant, and I caught him looking at Dawn and me a few too many times.

Dawn noticed the change in my attitude, and I saw this cause her to tense up as well. We finished our lunch mostly in silence while I snuck a few covert glances in the hotshot's direction. I also saw his mug stayed mostly full over the next twenty minutes; he obviously wasn't here for the beer.

I pulled out my phone and fumbled with it, stealthily taking a photo of the guy at the bar. Next, I tapped out a text without sending it, then passed it to Dawn to read as I laughed, like I was sharing something funny that I had been sent. She laughed too, letting me know she was on board with what I had planned. Then I sent a real text to Murph and waited on a reply. After it came we paid our tab and left. We walked down the covered breezeway between the *Beach Bar* and the *Catamaran Bar & Grill* over toward the marina. Just past the seafood steam shack, instead of continuing straight through charter boat row, we hung a right, down the private dock. I used a keycard to get through the security gate. After making sure it closed securely and sneaking a look back behind us while I did, we continued down the private dock and boarded *Predator*, our fifty-five-foot Jarrett Bay sportfisherman.

On my glance back at the gate, I had indeed spotted "Sport," the guy from *Wet Dream*, spying on us from behind the corner of the steam shack. No doubt about it; he'd been following us. So, my intuition about the guy had been right. We had come to *Predator* because we wanted the gate to provide some distance between us and the guy. Whatever he had planned, we didn't want to lead him over to *Lady Dawn* to try to pull it off there. I texted an update to Murph, who was now situated across the basin aboard our newly named *Incognito*. My earlier text had gone to him with a picture of "Sport" attached. He texted back that the guy was now at a table on the patio at *Mallard Cove Restaurant*, watching both the gate on the private dock as well as the marina basin, obviously waiting to see where we might go.

I called since Murph was far enough away from the guy not to be heard.

"Hey. Let's give 'Sport' an hour. If he doesn't leave by then, I'm going to go confront him. But since he's so interested in us or me and where we go, I'd love to follow him and return the favor. He's too much of an amateur to be part of Attanasio's crew. And Joey's dead, so he couldn't have sent him."

Murph asked, "Know anybody else that would have sent some muscle-headed jagoff after you?"

I said, "Not really. Well, maybe Cetta, but I don't think his cojones are that big. This guy definitely recognized me, and I don't remember ever seeing him before."

"It's not that hard to pull up your picture on the internet, Case."

"I guess. But you'd need a reason. Hey, what about that idiot yacht broker? We did tick him off this morning."

"I was the one who pissed him off the most, I'm out in plain sight and this guy hasn't given me a second glance," Murph said.

"Well, like I said, let's give him a little time and if he doesn't take off, I'll go have a chat with him. But I think we'll learn more if we find out where he came from, instead of challenging him face to face."

"Agreed. I'll let you know if things change."

ANGELA GREEN WAS a former nurse who had to change vocations after being caught stealing narcotics in her former job at a Charlottesville hospital. Her sad downhill slide due to her growing addiction had become a classic one as her nursing career quickly imploded. Wanting a change of scenery and hopeful that her past wouldn't follow her, she headed for the seashore and Virginia Beach.

What Angela found at the coast was a steady supply of pills, coke, and weed that all funneled through the Golden Gal strip club. It was also there where she eventually found her new line of work that provided a very good income, more than enough to buy the drugs she craved. With her fashion-model looks, she quickly grabbed Jimmy's attention, and he talked her into becoming the club's premier dancer.

As Jimmy's favorite, he quickly molded her into a useful "tool" for his business, of which the strip club was only a small part. His hold over her was cemented through his control of her drug supply. The job he gave her today was about to mark a major milestone in her downfall. But in Jimmy's eyes, it would make her so much more valuable to him.

Dressed in scrubs that had been left over from her days in Charlottesville, she nodded to the guard in the hall outside of Bobby's room. Fortunately, Bobby was asleep, and she silently moved over to the IV pole and located the medication port on the line. Taking a syringe out from under her scrub's top, she emptied the contents into the line with a smooth, continuous push of the plunger.

She watched Bobby's eyelids as they slowly opened, his eyes searching and finally focusing on her for a second. ""Ang..." It would be the last word he would ever attempt to say as the "hot-shot" started taking effect. Angela wiped down the syringe with alcohol, obliterating her fingerprints and any residual DNA, then dropped it in the "Sharps Disposal" container. She amazed herself with how calm she was; her hands weren't even shaking. Especially since she'd now taken the leap from being an angel of mercy to becoming the angel of death.

Once out in the hall, she again nodded to the guard and slowly made her way to the stairwell and down to the parking garage. She smiled as she thought about how pleased Jimmy was going to be, and more importantly, how he'd promised to make it worth her while.

"Sport's" attention span was fortunately short, and less than half an hour later he was on the move again. Casting off in his boat, he stared at the bow of *Predator* as he passed by, then refocused on navigating the basin's inlet.

Murph maneuvered the bow of *Incognito* up to the end of the finger pier next to *Predator*, and I climbed aboard. I had changed clothes, donned wrap-around sunglasses and now wore a large-brimmed canvas fishing hat that shaded my face. With this getup, I doubt that "Sport" could recognize me from farther than ten yards away, and I didn't plan on getting even that close. We couldn't risk taking Dawn along; with her height as well as her flaming red hair, she stood out no matter where she went. And despite this being a custom boat, with no name and a plain white hull, from a distance *Incognito* resembled so many production center consoles. We were as inconspicuous as possible, just like we needed to be.

I took the helm from Murph. As we cleared the marina's inlet we could see the red speedboat off in the distance, looking like it was making a beeline for Lynnhaven Inlet across the mouth of the bay. Fortunately, after hitting wide-open-throttle when he left *Mallard Cove*, "Sport" had quickly throttled back to a more economical cruising speed, and we had no problem following him at a distance. Running parallel to the CBBT bridges, we could see that the north-bound lanes were shut down, probably due to an accident some-where closer to Lynnhaven. We covered the seventeen miles to the inlet in a little over half an hour, and we never saw "Sport" look back even once.

The ocean had just a slight roll to it, less than two feet, and *Incognito* barely felt it. Even with only having spent a total of around an hour running her, I was already in love with the way she handled and rode. Of course, the true test of how she handles will come on a rough day. But I had no doubt that with her deep entry forward, wide beam, and Carolina style wide-flared bow, she'd still handle a large sea just fine.

As we neared the shore I sped up a little, closing the gap between us to less than a quarter-mile. I wasn't as concerned with being spotted now since this far away he probably wouldn't suspect that our boat had also come from *Mallard Cove*. Lynnhaven has a decent amount of traffic in the summer even during mid-week, and today was no exception.

It was a good thing that I had moved closer because once inside the inlet there are several channels to choose from, not to mention dozens of bays and coves. "Sport" took the first channel on the left, the one that took him closest to the Pilot boat's docks and the larger waterfront restaurants and bars. It was the latter that I'm sure influenced his choice of channel, as he could scan the tables closest to the water to make sure both he and his gaudy floating billboard were being seen as he passed by.

I opted for the channel farther in from the inlet, knowing from experience that the two would converge ahead. This way we can slip right in behind him again, without him having a clue as to who we are or where we had come from. Already at a fast idle, I backed off the throttle even further to ensure that he reached the convergence point first. We had a great view of his bright red hull from our channel as we were on a parallel course only a couple of hundred yards apart, and there was no problem tracking him. After the two channels merged, he continued east, bearing to the right at the tip of Bay Island before passing under the Great Neck bridges. Going left here would have taken us toward our Lynnhaven project, and I was relieved that wasn't our destination.

A quarter-mile or so beyond the big bridge he turned left into a private channel. This one curved around inside a large sandbar and up against the shore and private docks of Bay Island. We stayed in the main channel, still having a perfect view of his movements without catching his attention. We watched as he slowed and approached the dock at a house on its own private peninsula. A mid-sized express sportfisherman named *Polecat* lay stern-out in a slip on the far side of the dock. But "Sport" headed for a submerged boat lift on the nearer side. This was an odd setup since the dock was way off to the side of the property, with both boats completely out of view from the house. Most boat owners like being able to look at their boats, if nothing else for security's sake.

At the base of the dock was a parking area, and a bright metallic gold Escalade was the only car sitting there. With as loud as the paint was, I had little doubt this was "Sport's" ride. I had Murph take some covert shots with his phone as we passed by, even though we were over a hundred yards away. Once past this point, Broad Bay opened up in front of us, and I was able to get us back up to cruising speed.

On the off-chance that "Sport" might have been watching, I ran *Incognito* over to the boat ramps at the far end of the bay at First Landing State Park, roughly a mile ahead. This way it would look like I was dropping off or picking up a passenger at the parking lot there. By the time that we turned around and ran back, *Wet Dream* was high and dry and the gaudy Escalade was missing.

I called Dawn on speakerphone to bring her up to date, and tell her we were headed back. By that time I had begun to doubt that this guy had any sinister intentions, and I admitted that to her.

"Case, I've never known your intuition to be far off, and I felt he was really, well... creepy."

"Yeah, but he could've been interested in you; maybe he just has a thing for redheads. So, the question is whether he is creepy in a 'meat-market-pickup-bar-guy' kind of creepy, or dangerous creepy?"

"Maybe both. You've got pictures of him and his house so why not send them to Rikki and see what she can find out. After what you've been through lately, you need to be extra careful right now."

Murph agreed. "It can't hurt to be cautious. Just because the guy has an expensive house and rides doesn't mean he's not a crook of some sort."

"Okay, I'll forward them to Rik. I guess we all felt strongly enough at the time to follow the guy all the way back here, so there must be something to it."

I hung up with Dawn and surrendered the helm to Murph. I tapped out a long text to Rik then sent the pictures. I was surprised to get a call back a couple of minutes later.

Rikki said, "I was about to call you when you texted. Your shooter's dead."

"I thought Dave only hit him in the shoulder!"

"He did. The guy didn't die from the gunshot, somebody snuck into the hospital and injected a lethal dose of narcotics into his IV."

For the second time today, the hair on the back of my neck stood up. I explained what we'd seen and done, then sent her the pictures while we talked. By the time we hung up, I noticed we were almost back to Lynnhaven Inlet. I also saw that Murph had a big smile on his face, so I didn't make any move to take back the helm.

"I hope this ends up being a whole lot of nothing," I said.

"Well, whatever it is, at least it got me a fun run on this rig. Skip must've been just sick over being forced to sell her, she's one sweet ride."

I nodded. "I lucked out on this one. Thanks for your help with getting rid of that weasel broker."

"No problem. Now, we need to get cranking on our brokerage," Murph said.

"You were serious about that," I asked?

"Heck yeah, weren't you? There's money to be made there, especially as we build a reputation for dealing honestly. We just need to find some good salespeople."

I said, "I thought you had your hands full with the catamaran business?" Murph had invested in ESVACats, a production catamaran manufacturing and sailboat racing technology company based up at Kari's cousin Carlton Albury's boatyard on Magothy Bay.

"Nah, Dickie has recovered well enough that he doesn't need as much help from me now. So, Linds and I both have time to devote to creating another business. I want to keep following your lead, investing in new properties and building businesses where I can empower people who can run them for me."

Murph's partner Dickie had been attacked, leaving him with a temporary mobility impairment. Murph had been taking up the slack for him.

"That's all good news. Yes, I'm ready to jump into that with you, especially if we can get the right people for it," I said.

Murph nodded, "I have a few in mind. I can't wait to kick that Jim Smith guy in the wallet. He deserves it for trying to take advantage of

Skip when he was down. I'll make some calls this afternoon and get things rolling."

~

As he walked in, Tony Pro saw Angela snorting up a long, fat line of cocaine on the side table next to the couch in Jimmy's office. Jimmy was behind his desk, looking a lot more secure and happy now than he had when Tony left.

"What'd you find out about this Shaw guy," Jimmy asked.

Tony replied, "I found him and that broad he's engaged to. Man, she's some kind of looker. Bobby was right, they're livin' on a boat over there, a sportfish. I couldn't get down the dock, they've got a security gate you need a key for. But I got a look at the name on the bow, *Predator.*"

"What do ya mean you saw it from the bow?"

"I took my boat. The CBBT was backed up, some kinda wreck or somethin'."

"What the hell did you do that for? You might as well have taken out a freakin' billboard that says, 'hey, look at me!' So much for keepin' a low profile like I told ya to."

"Nobody cared, Jimmy, they didn't pay any attention to it. And Shaw never looked twice at me."

"So then, Mr. Invisible, how're we supposed to get to Shaw?" Jimmy was still irritated with Tony.

"I figure we sneak in by tyin' up to the dock inside a that gate, then we get onboard and snatch his chick. She ought to be worth a hundred grand to him, easy. And with a rig like that he might even have that much just layin' around."

"Risky. What else ya got?"

"Uh, that's it. We grab her and ransom her back."

From across the room came a long sniff. Not Angela snorting another line, but her disapproving of the plan. Both men looked over at her, Tony very irritatingly. But Jimmy looked like she had his attention.

"What is it?"

She smiled, and pinched both nostrils together, not in comment to Tony's plan, but to capture some errant powder that was trying to escape. Then she said, "Why are you getting all worked up about how you're going to get around some security fence thing?"

Tony said condescendingly, "Because, sweet cheeks, we need to get to the girl to snatch her. And speaking of snatches, why don't you get yours out there on stage and make us some money."

Jimmy held up his hand, "Shut up, Tony. You've got an idea, Angela?"

Tony exploded, "Wait Jimmy, you're gonna ask her for..."

Jimmy slammed his hand down on his desk as he glared at Tony, "What part of 'shut up' don't you get?" He looked back at Angela. "What's your idea?"

She smiled, "Why try to get *in* to get at the girl when it's a lot easier to get the guy to come *out*, to get at another one. You say this guy's engaged, right?"

Jimmy smiled at her as what she was saying started making sense. "Right."

"Honey, we make a fortune off bachelor parties, a lot of it off the grooms. If there's one thing I know about guys, it's that they can't turn down one last screw before they say, 'I do.' So, don't worry about getting in, that's his job. Bobby said they were *both* loaded, right? So, it doesn't matter which one we grab." She smiled wickedly as she picked up the small mirror and then snorted another line as Jimmy laughed.

Tony scowled, he didn't like being overruled, especially by some stripper. He wanted to change the subject quickly, to try and get his authority back. "So Jimmy, what're we gonna do about Bobby?"

"It's been handled."

"Whattaya mean?"

"You heard him, it's *handled*. So you don't need to worry your little head about it," Angela said, smiling condescendingly.

Suddenly Tony understood where this new crappy attitude of Angela's was coming from, and he was alarmed. It hit him that Jimmy must've given her the big pile of coke that was on the mirror as a bonus. Usually, he was only that generous after he got laid by one of the strippers, or somebody did a job for him. But most of the time when he knocked off a piece, afterward he just wanted the chick out of the office, pronto. Instead, Angela looked like she was making herself at home. Meaning, she must've solved Jimmy's 'Bobby problem.' Also meaning that he had greatly underestimated this chick and that she was a real threat, way smarter and more dangerous than he had given her credit for.

While this worried Tony that his place in the organization might be being undermined by her, he also figured he couldn't be replaced. Plus he knew that everybody had a demon they couldn't control. She came here looking for a supply of drugs, and that's one thing he had easy access to. Jimmy would be careful not to give her more than she could handle, but Tony could tip that scale and help her destroy herself. And that was now his plan.

16

CRYSTAL

After we got back to *Mallard Cove*, we went aboard *Lady Dawn*. Her namesake joined us, anxious to hear more details about what we had seen. She brought her tablet with her and pulled up the satellite view of Bay Island while I filled her in on everything including the death of our shooter.

I sat on the couch next to her as she asked, "Which house was it?"

Looking at it from the overhead view, I couldn't tell. "Not sure."

Murph pointed it out, "This one."

That was when Dawn noticed that he had sat down next to her on the couch, in the closest proximity they'd been to each other since their breakup. She glared at him for a second but didn't say anything. More evidence of her starting to forgive him. Maybe. She pulled up the owner's information for the house which was registered to a James Impasato. Then my phone rang, it was Rikki.

"That house you sent me the picture of?"

I interrupted, "Let me guess, it belongs to James Impasato."

"All right smartass, do you know who 'James' is?"

"Uh, sorry Rik, no I don't. But I'm guessing he's bad news if you're calling."

"He's better known as 'Jimmy the Eye.' Virginia Beach police have been trying to nail him for years, but he's too slippery, always a step ahead. He has the whole town wired. Operates out of his strip club, the Golden Gal. Drugs, loan sharking, escorts, and lately the odd contract murder. Your shooter was his cousin Bobby. Jimmy was probably the one who ordered him killed so that he couldn't cut a deal. Blood isn't thicker than water with this bunch, and he's protected by Attanasio."

"Wow, what a cold one. But also what an ego, running around in that go-fast and a gold Escalade, you can't miss him."

"Those aren't his, they belong to his lieutenant, 'Tony Pro' Giamatti, and he's the guy in the picture you sent me. He keeps his boat on Jimmy's lift. Not the brightest bulb on the tree, but one of the most ambitious. If he was scouting you out, it means that you're on Jimmy's radar for some reason. Maybe he blames you for his cousin getting caught and then silenced. Or, maybe it wasn't Joey that had the contract out on you after all, though that certainly made sense."

I said, "Hey!"

"I mean in a logical view of things, not that it should've been done."

"Thanks for clearing that up," I said dryly.

She continued, "But what doesn't make sense is that the contract should've died with Joey if it was his. There should've been no reason for Tony Pro to be stalking you, especially out in the open like that."

She was right, about all of it. And if this guy was far up the ladder in "Jimmy the Eye's" organization and he was about to make an attempt on my life, you would think he'd be a bit more subtle than to show up in such an attention-grabbing, floating "Johnson extender."

I said, "Maybe he's not as bright as he thinks he is."

"Well if he was trying to send you a message, there are far better ways to do it. But you want me to send Dave back down there, just in case?"

"I don't think that's necessary. We all know what this guy looks like, and we'll be watching for him. I'll ask Murph to get a copy of his picture to all the marina and restaurant staff, too."

"Okay, but keep your eyes open. I don't like how this feels."

I replied, "Will do Rik, thanks. Don't worry, we've got this."

PAULIE ATTANASIO WAS FURIOUS AGAIN. "Why is it dat the smallest part of my territory is the biggest pain in my ass? Is everybody down dere a moron or what? Now Jimmy whacked his own cousin? First, he tries to take out a Fed for Joey, now he pulls dis. He's gotta be stopped, he doesn't have enough brains to run that operation. And his strip club has gotten too much of a high profile now, it's gotta go, too. Make that guy with the other club a deal, but let him know, no branchin' out on his own like Jimmy did. He works for us, no sidelines unless they're approved."

His lieutenant nodded and hurried out of Paulie's office. He knew he had to get this done, or it would be on his head, too. If Jimmy had only played it smart, he'd have kept a good thing going. Now, it was going to bury him.

AFTER MURPH LEFT, Bimini, Dawn, and I went over to the Cove Club, checking on its progress. All the docks were now floating in place and tied together. A Hydrocrane with a pile driver was setting the huge steel pipes that they would permanently pin them in place, allowing them to ride up and down with the tides.

Concrete footers were also being poured for the "L" shaped carport area columns. This cover is being built beside *Lady Dawn's* slip then will turn and run behind all the other slips over to the boathouse. A backhoe was busy digging a trench for power and water that would supply the docks, boathouse, and C2. At the rate things were going, they'd have the asphalt in and the slips ready in a week or two. About the same time that Bimini will have finally "watered" every last bush and tree within the fenced area, warning every critter on ESVA that this is *his* home. After twenty minutes of flat-out running and intermittent stops, he came trotting back up to us, having once again totally emptied his bladder. He plopped down in between the two of us with a contented sigh.

I looked at him and asked, "Perimeter marked and secure?"

He glared up at me and looked back down. As I've said before, dogs can glare, and this one knows when he's being teased.

"Pay no attention to your dad, Bim. I appreciate your efforts at making us secure," Dawn told him. In reply, he rolled on his side against her ankle and "chuffed" in my direction. Yes, he not only glares, but sometimes gets in the last word too.

My phone "binged" with an incoming text. Murph, wanting to meet up at the *Catamaran* bar in half an hour to go over the brokerage plans. I invited Dawn, but she already had Lindsay and Kari coming over for after-work cocktails on *Lady Dawn*.

I looked at Bim, "It's dog friendly, pal."

He lifted his head, looked at me, then promptly lay it back down, this time with his snout across Dawn's foot.

"Pretty sure that's a 'no,' Case."

"Yeah, more like an 'I'm staying home with mom and the girls,' Dawn."

THE *CATAMARAN* OR *"THE CAT"* as it's better known, is another open-air beach bar on the other side of the breezeway from the *Mallard Cove Beach Bar*. Both had been Kari's idea, but the *Cat* was added after the *Beach Bar* had become a huge hit, especially with the sportfish crowd, and they needed more bar space.

Powerboaters and sailors don't always mix well, so Kari had come up with the *Cat* to cater to the sailing crowd. The two long benches that flanked the bar were actually inverted catamaran hulls that had come from an early ESVACat prototype. Old ESVACat sails were attached to the roof rafters.

The truth is, I don't care which bar I drink in, or what method of propulsion I'm using. I just like being on or beside the water. But if I'm beside it, having a drink in hand is usually a plus.

I spotted Murph over in the far corner, at my favorite table in the bar. He already had two beers waiting, so I knew he had a lot to tell me. He started in before I even finished sitting down.

"We can use the space next door to Timmy's bait shop; there's nothing in there but some old junk that needs to go out anyway," Murph said.

I asked, "Isn't that kind of small?"

"You want to put more money in office rent to our partners, or have a larger and better advertising budget? All we need is a place that looks good enough for closings and looks expensive enough so that we look like we know what we're doing without also looking like we're gouging our clients."

"Murph, who is this 'we' you keep referring to? I don't have time to be a boat broker."

"I figured we'd find someone who's an old hand at it who's also looking to make a change. I run across some boats for sale every now and then, so I wouldn't mind being a bit 'hands-on.' Might make a fun sideline for me, flipping boats."

I said, "So long as you don't mean literally."

"Funny guy. I've done pretty well at it you know."

I did know. He'd hustled a few boat deals after leaving Bayside, bumping him and Lindsay up into bigger and better boats. Then a huge white marlin tournament purse had given him enough cash to start pursuing real estate deals, *Mallard Cove* being his first. Yeah, he was a first-class hustler when he wanted to be, and this brokerage was starting to look like it would do well by it.

Two beers in, we had a pretty detailed 'bar napkin list' going, and a plan. Then Murph said, "Hey, I'll be back in a minute. You can never buy beer, just rent it you know." He made his way across the open-air bar, signaling our server for two more beers while he went to make room for his next one.

I was thinking over what we discussed when I heard, "Is this seat taken?" I looked up into a pair of emerald green eyes that were attached to a very attractive twenty-something-year-old blonde. She was wearing cutoff blue jeans and a low buttoned fishing shirt that barely hid some breathtaking curves. She was in the process of sitting down in Murph's seat before I could collect my thoughts enough to answer her. I'd be lying if I said I wasn't distracted by her...shirt. Most guys would have been.

"Uh, yes, it kind of is."

"Well, you're right. By me. I'm Crystal." She flashed an overly whitened set of beautiful teeth and held out her hand, which I left hanging.

"And I'm flattered, but I'm also engaged, Crystal."

"Well, there's engaged, and then there's *engaged*. And in my book, that also means you aren't married. Though you look like you'd be worth it even if you were. But no ring means fair game."

Any man would be an idiot not to be flattered. But any man who thinks with his large head first would know to get the hell away from "Crystal" or risk becoming an even bigger idiot.

"Again, I'm flattered, but I'm just not in the market. Have a great day, Crystal, but you need to go find somewhere else to sit."

"You don't know what you're missing Ca...fella. We could have a lot of fun together, the two of us." She looked a bit shocked, and also a bit insulted.

"Thanks for the thought, but again, I'll pass."

She got up and walked away, pausing a few steps later to give an over-the-shoulder glance to see if I was watching her as she did. Okay, I'm a partial idiot because I was. Wait, had she started to call me Casey?

"Not a bad view there, Casey. I think I'll have a beer to go with it."

The person who said that was now sitting down in the chair across from Murph's.

"A beer does go well with it, Sandy. How's it going?" I motioned to our server for a beer for Sandy.

"It's going great. I should've gotten out of *Bayside* last season. This place is a goldmine of characters, plots, and subplots. Take her for instance. Zeroed in on you like a torpedo. She's just lucky a certain redhead wasn't here to blow her out of the water." He grinned, having seen Dawn's "redhead pissed" side once or twice over the last year.

"Don't I know it, which is why I tried to send her packing as fast as I could."

"Geeze, what is it with you guys, we gotta drink in a 'blow-boater' bar now?" Baloney had arrived, taking the chair across from Sandy.

Sandy snorted, "Since when do you care, so long as there's somebody else's tab to put your beers on, shorty?"

"I told you ta quit callin' me that, ya beer mooch!"

"Yeah, well, if the inseam fits..."

"I see the afternoon's entertainment has arrived." Murph was back, and he slid into his chair just as our server brought the beer.

"Nothin' entertaining about *him*," Bill glared at Sandy who smirked in return, further irritating him.

Sandy said, "No, you missed the *real* entertainment." He went on to tell the story about the blonde girl.

"Oh yeah, I saw her at the bar, talking with some Spanish looking dude. Sandy's right, it's a good thing for her that Dawn wasn't around," Murph said.

Fortunately, the conversation quickly shifted to fishing, since for me the sooner the blonde was forgotten, the better. Gossip has a way of getting around a marina and usually gets embellished. I'll be sure to tell Dawn about it when I get back to the boat. It's not that she doesn't trust me and vice versa, but then she's prepared to shut it down if someone brings up Crystal.

By the end of this beer, it was time for me to make more room for another. "I've got to hit the head. Order me another, would you Murph?" He nodded.

The bathrooms are down the breezeway and to the left, along a walkway that leads to the *Cove* restaurant's parking lot. I was just coming back out when I heard an argument. The blonde and the Spanish looking guy were on the walkway, fighting. The man slapped her hard, and she went down. I leapt at the guy, grabbing his wrists. He broke one loose and pulled a pistol out of his back waistband. As I was reaching for my own pistol, I felt the barrel of a gun in my back. A hand then removed my pistol from its holster.

"Head for the parking lot. *MOVE!*" The blonde shoved me while she kept me covered from behind with her pistol. I glanced back, and the barrel was again jammed painfully into my back. "I said *MOVE!*"

As we emerged from the walkway, the car that was in the closest parking space was a black Dodge Charger Hellcat. The Spanish guy went ahead and opened the back driver's side door. The blonde said, "Get in and slide across."

Damn. I was hoping to get the seat behind the driver, where he couldn't target me with his gun, too. That way if I could overpower and disarm the blonde, I could at least shoot the driver through the back of his seat. But by being on the passenger's side, he'd have a clear shot at me between the two bucket seat-backs.

"Call your sweetie," the blonde instructed. "One false move or say anything stupid, and you get a bullet in your knee, and you'll need a new one, got it?" When I nodded she continued, "Tell her to get together a hundred grand in twenties and put it in a gym bag. Then put another fifty grand in a second bag. No tracers or dye packs. We'll call her again tomorrow morning with instructions on where to make the drop. No calling the cops either, or you're a dead man. Am I making myself clear?"

I nodded, then slowly reached for my phone as we exited the parking lot. We headed north, away from the CBBT as I called Dawn.

"Hey, when are you headed back, I thought we'd..."

"Hold it, I've been kidnapped, Dawn. This is no joke. I can see by the looks on the faces of these two 'stay here's' they're dead serious."

The blonde didn't like my running off script and she yelled, "Just tell the bitch what to do!"

I gave her the instructions and had her repeat them back. Then she said, "I'll have to get the cash from the bank in the morning so they need to give me that much time. And they don't get the money until I talk to you again before I leave for the drop." Calm, cool, and thinking fast. God, how I love this woman.

I said, "Just get the money together as fast as you can. The bank manager, Rikki, can help you. Her private number is written in my datebook. I love you."

"I love you too, Case. Don't worry, I'll get Rikki to help me, and we'll get you back here soon."

The bit about seeing her "back here" was just to let me know she'd picked up on my "stay here" reference. Not "born here" or "come here," she understood we were staying here, as in on ESVA. There were only two directions to take out of that parking lot, south across the bridges to VA Beach, or north to somewhere on ESVA. I also let her know there were two of them, and I'd seen both of their faces. Meaning, they couldn't afford to let me live and possibly testify against them. She picked up on that too, telling them without talking to me tomorrow, she wouldn't hand over the money. Now she'd call Rikki, and hopefully, she'll be able to find us, wherever it is that we're headed.

The blonde took my smartphone, cracked her window, and dropped it out onto the roadway. I looked back and watched as it tumbled and broke into pieces at sixty miles-per-hour. That was one less tool that Rikki now had to track us. I prayed that she had more in her bag of tricks.

17

NEW MANAGEMENT

"Man, that friend of yours is one lucky dog, Murph. First I seen him around with that killer-looking Ginger, an' just now he left with Crystal!" Willie was a local boatman who picked up work along the docks. He had walked up to the table to say hello to the three of them, always doing a little PR work to keep his name out there in case they ever needed any work done on their boats.

"Who are you talking about, Willie?"

"That guy on the Hargrave, whazziz name, Casey?"

Murph was confused, "Who's Crystal?"

"The hottest babe around, that's who! Pretty gal in cutoff jeans and a fishing shirt, with a body that oughta be continued on the next gal. I know fer sure, 'cause I seen her buck ass nekkid before."

"And Casey was leaving with her?"

"Yeah, him an' some other guy, but Casey was getting' in the back-seat a the car with her, a black Charger Hellcat. That car's almost as hot as Crystal! Ain't many of them around."

"So, you used to date her?"

"Hell, don't I wish! Nah, she's a dancer over at Golden Gal in VA Beach. Let me tell you, I'd love to trade places with that dancin' pole, ya know what I mean?" He gave Murph a nudge and a knowing leer before he ambled off to chat with other potential customers up at the bar.

Murph was still confused when his phone rang, and he was shocked to see that it was Dawn since she never called him. "Uh, hey Dawn?"

"Murph, did you see Casey leave?"

Alarmed that Dawn might've already heard that Casey had left with the blond, Murph decided to lie for his friend. "I think he's around here somewhere?"

"No, he's not. I need you over here at my boat right now. Run, and I mean don't stop for anything!" She hung up.

Sandy and Baloney looked amused, having overheard the conversation, but not having caught onto Dawn's tone, though Murph had. It wasn't angry, it was more grave, at least as close to grave as Dawn ever got. She's normally very upbeat.

"Have them put this on my tab, I gotta go," Murph said as he jumped up and made for the door.

Baloney looked at Sandy, "I don't know about you, but I'm sure Murph meant for us to have another round or two on him."

Sandy replied, "You're such a beer scrounge!" As Bill started to scowl at him he continued, "But it would be impolite for me to leave you sitting here drinking all by yourself, short stuff, so if you insist, I guess I'll have to stay here and beer-sit you."

Baloney started to object until he caught the "beer-sit" reference. Then he grinned and held up two fingers at their server. "Ya know, for a boring-assed writer with a huge-assed ego, you can be okay at times. Not allatime, but sometimes." He grinned as he leaned back in his chair.

MURPH DIDN'T BOTHER KNOCKING, he just barged into the salon where Dawn was on the phone with Rikki. Kari had already left to meet up with Marlin after a couple of drinks, but Lindsay was still there with

Dawn so Murph sat with her. He caught the gist of Dawn's side of the conversation, and even after everything that had happened the last few weeks, he was shocked. He interrupted her.

"Put it on speakerphone." After Dawn did that he related what had happened at the table and what Willie had said, including that the girl was a dancer at the Golden Gal.

"'Jimmy the Eye' again," Dawn said.

"Sounds like it. I doubt any of his group would take this on by themselves," Rikki said. "Interesting they didn't head over to VA Beach though, where I'm sure Jimmy would have had a lot more contacts. Only one main road over here on ESVA and that's an attention-getting car."

Dawn asked, "Should I call the sheriff? He gave us his direct number."

Rikki discouraged her. "The sheriff didn't even know what Lonnano was up to. We know Jimmy has the VA Beach police wired, there's little or no reason not to assume that if he's got a stash house over here, he probably has someone in the sheriff's office here, too. Calling him could easily get Casey killed. So no, we handle this 'in house.' My house."

"Not without us," Murph said.

"I know you want to help, Murph. But just let me handle this. Remember, my team are all pros. So, the first thing we need to do is find where Casey's being held. Then we'll figure out how to get him back. We need to be sure that we don't tip them off in the process. I'll get my team working on that," Rikki said.

Dawn asked, "Should I plan on getting the money together in the morning?"

Rik replied, "Let's worry about that if we can't find him by then. That was an awesome move, telling her that if you don't talk to Casey then, there's no leaving for the drop. Our best chance at getting Case back alive and well is before any drop is supposed to happen."

"Because he has seen their faces?"

"I'm afraid so, Dawn."

Murph asked, "So, you're saying they can't let him go. I mean alive, right?"

"No, Murph, they won't. So we have to find him before then. Sit tight, I'll call you back as soon as I know something."

THERE IS GOING to be no getting out of here alive for me if they have their way, I know that. Not only had they let me see their faces, but I was able to see exactly where we went, and I can easily find it again. My guess is they plan on killing me here, in this old boarded-up warehouse office a few hundred yards off the main road near Cape Charles. My ankles and knees are bound with duct tape, as are my hands. At least my arms are in front of me instead of behind my back. But the only way I would be able to move around would be like an inchworm, and my captors are both here in the office with me. While I'm sitting against a wall, they are at a table across this small room. They're snorting lines of cocaine every twenty minutes or so, and babbling to each other non-stop.

As darkness had fallen outside, the drug's paranoia stage had kicked in. Any perceived noise now sends one or the other racing over to the only window to peer through a small space between the boards on the outside that cover it. The only light in the room is coming from a small lamp on the table, near where they're chopping their coke.

Through their conversation, I've been able to garner from it that this is Jimmy the Eye's operation. I also found out that he wasn't aware of that second bag with the fifty grand; these two are double-crossing him.

I've managed to take a few brief catnaps throughout the evening. I know that Rikki and her team are right now moving heaven and earth to find me, and I need to be as rested as possible when they do. And I have no doubt that they will. I can't doubt them, it's the only way I can see I'll be able to get out of here alive.

The two cokeheads are both as wired as they can be right now, but from the sound of it, they are running low on their stash. They intend to stay up all night and then do the drop, but that isn't going to happen without more coke. Crystal said she should have a quarter ounce waiting back at the club that Tony Pro promised he'd stash there for her, and she wants to run down to get it. Her partner isn't keen on the idea, being left alone with me and without a vehicle. She managed to convince him this was the only way they would be able to stay awake all night and still get the job done.

I'm guessing that it's now well after midnight, and roundtrip to VA Beach and back was going to be somewhere around two hours. No doubt Crystal would hit some of the stash before the return trip, and in the meantime, her partner would be on the downside of his wired high. If I can somehow manage to get loose, I might have a chance to take him. But soon after Crystal left, his paranoia amplified, as did his need to communicate. He started rambling to me about how he planned to eventually take over Jimmy's operation, and how Angela would end up with him, not Jimmy. I guess that's "Crystal's" real name. Great, I've been kidnapped by a lovestruck cokehead with dreams of grandeur. If I get half a chance, I'm going to put an end to all his dreams. Permanently.

A HALF-HOUR later Rikki called Dawn with news.

"Okay, we know where they've taken Casey." Rikki was on speakerphone again. "We couldn't find anything in Jimmy Impasato's name. The Golden Gal business is held in a Limited Liability Corporation, with some VA Beach lawyer listed as the Registered Agent. It's the only thing that LLC owns, it doesn't even own the real estate, which is in another LLC with that same Registered Agent. We did a search and there are a dozen similar LLC's connected with that guy. We went through each one of those and only found one that owns any real estate on ESVA, an old warehouse up near Cape Charles.

"I sent one of our guys over to scout it, and he spotted the Charger in the back of the building. I've got him sitting in the adjoining woods, keeping eyeballs on it. There are only two doors and a single window in the place. We'll wait until dark then see if we can't get a look inside with an endoscope camera. Then we'll make a plan to breach it and get Casey out."

Murph spoke up, "Then we have to do something about Impasato, or he'll pull something again."

"One thing at a time, Murph, but yes, we're going to deal with him. But let's just get Casey home first."

TONY PRO WAS the last one left in the Golden Gal after the club closed at two a.m. He was placing the last of the night's cash receipts in the office safe when he heard a noise behind him. He never saw the two-by-four coming that connected with the side of his head as he turned.

When Tony regained consciousness, he realized he was gagged and duct-taped to the center stage dance pole. Two guys were in the room, talking together.

"I killed all the circuits but these lights at the breaker panel, so there won't be anything else to set it off."

"Good. Go ahead and open the valves and let's get the hell out of here." The one who said that started to walk by Tony when he noticed he was awake. "Ah, Tony, back from your nap, eh? Hey, sorry 'bout this. But you know how it is, nothin' personal, just business. An' Jimmy's been a little too sloppy lately, so Paulie's doin' a little bit of reorganizing. You just got caught in the middle. Crappy luck, huh."

The club now reeked of gasoline, and as the other man opened the valve on the first of four propane canisters in the room, the realization of what they had planned dawned on Tony. He started screaming behind the gag, but only a muffled whimper escaped. And the tape job had left him totally unable to move, he could only stand upright like a mummified totem pole.

"Ah, don' worry. When Jimmy gets here and opens the door, it'll all be over. And you had a good run while it lasted. I guess I'll see youse in hell." He went to the back entrance of the club that the staff used and attached the device. Then he and his accomplice went out the front door, his partner using Tony's keys to lock the door behind them. A quick squirt of five-minute epoxy in the keyhole made sure the only way into the club now was through that back entrance. He said to his partner, "You know, I never liked that dumb prick, Tony."

"But it's almost three a.m.," Jimmy the Eye protested.

"Tell me aboudit. An' I gotta long drive back ahead a me. You're not makin' it go any faster, either. I'll meet you in your office in twenty minutes. Make sure you leave the back door unlocked so's I can get in."

Jimmy knew what this must be about. Paulie must've figured out that Jimmy was holding back some of the "taste," the percentage of profits that was supposed to go to Jersey, and he was sending his guy for a face-to-face. He could never admit to shorting Paulie or he'd be a dead man, but he'd have to listen to whatever the message is. Maybe this was something that could be squared with a nice cash bundle that the guy could take back north to Paulie.

Fifteen minutes later he pulled up to the club and spotted Crystal's car in the back. That was wrong, it shouldn't be here, and neither should she. Crystal was just putting her key in the back door when he saw her. Jimmy was pissed, he should never have given her that key. She was supposed to be up at Cape Charles, babysitting that Shaw guy. There was only one reason for her to be here, she must have a stash somewhere in the club. You can never fully depend on a damn cokehead.

Crystal became wide-eyed as she recognized Jimmy's car. She paused for a second and considered going over to meet him as he got out like everything was fine, but she knew she was too wired to pull that off. He'd be pissed that she was here instead of at the warehouse, and about her being high. She turned and tugged on the club door just as the world erupted.

From his car Jimmy watched as a fireball blew open the door, engulfing Crystal as it threw her across the parking lot. Another fireball blew out the front door, the only other opening in the exterior of the building. The roof back by the office ruptured upward and then caved back in on itself as the trusses collapsed. The remaining trusses now fell like dominoes down past where Tony Pro's lifeless body remained. The wood and asphalt shingles began feeding the fire that surrounded Tony, soon making his dental records the best way to identify what would be left of him.

Jimmy jumped out of his car and raced across to Crystal. Most of her hair had been burned off of her head, and on one side of her face the skin had been burned and melted away, and that eye was now sightless. She moaned and wheezed, somehow having survived the blast, but not for long. The wheezing came from her lungs being seared by the fire's heat, able now to function at only a fraction of normal. Soon they would start filling up with fluid as her body begins fighting against the burns. Right now she was numb with shock, but if by some miracle she managed to keep on living, she'd soon be in agony.

Partly out of compassion, and partly to ensure that she would never be able to testify against him on the slim chance that she did live, Jimmy decided to end things. He used his thirty-eight caliber derringer pocket gun and shot her in the temple. He didn't realize it, but she saved his life not once but twice tonight. First by being the one to open the door, and second by his taking the time to check on her.

Paulie's guys had parked down the street, waiting to make sure their job was done. They recognized Jimmy's car as he arrived, and figured he was the one who opened the door. After he didn't reappear out front of the building, they were sure the explosion had done its job. Tomorrow they had a second job, to fill Jimmy's spot. A couple more days in this town, then back to Jersey. Neither one could wait to get back.

RIKKI and five of her team were now huddled out of earshot of the building at the wood's edge as one of them updated the rest on what the camera had revealed. There had been more than enough of a gap at the bottom of the door to snake the camera in for a look.

"Rikki, there's only one of the kidnappers in there, a male, about thirty. Shaw's against the far wall, sitting upright on the floor. The kidnapper keeps going over to the window and peering out every few minutes."

Fortunately, the road in front of the warehouse was seldom used, and the nearest house was over a quarter-mile away. This kept the kidnapper from totally freaking out since no cars were passing by, and it provided them some cover. It also gave Rikki an idea.

I THOUGHT I just heard a noise like a cat scratching at the window. Wait, there it is again. My captor also heard it, and he crept up to the glass, pistol in hand. As he leaned forward to peer between the two boards, the back of his head exploded as bits of bone, hair and gray matter mixed in a red mist that showered the area behind where he stood. The window glass breaking made more noise than the gun with the silencer that had delivered the bullet.

His body had barely landed on the floor when the door was kicked in. The first person through the door removed the kidnapper's weapon, not that he'd ever be using it again. The second person through the door was Rikki, who raced over to me, cutting me loose.

She said with a grin, "The things I have to do to get a fishing invitation out of you."

I said shakily, "What the hell took you so long?" Then I matched her grin, to let her know I was really okay. "There's another, and she'll be coming back soon."

"No worries, we put a tracker on her car, and we have someone following her. She's almost back to the strip club. We need to get out of here now, this was a 'lone ranger' kind of op, with no 'local yokels' in on it. You can never be too careful, especially after your run-in with Lonnano. No real way to tell who might be on Impasato's payroll. So, we'll torch this place to take care of any evidence, and to send your buddy Jimmy another lesson."

It felt weird, being on the right side of the law and yet still having to work in the shadows. But after what I'd been through, it didn't bother me *that* much. The law and order guys who were supposed to have been on my side had been more interested in politics than justice. I wasn't about to give them another shot at me. And the guy on the floor was going to kill me, so I had no compunction about him being shot and now torching his body.

Rᴉᴋ ᴅʀᴏᴠᴇ me straight back to the boat, and Dawn met me at the door with an embrace I'll never forget. When she finally unwrapped her arms from around me and we went inside, I saw Murph and Lindsay were still here. All three had been under the very watchful eye of Dave, who came over to give me a one-armed man-hug and a slap on the back. Rik stayed outside, as she'd gotten a call just as we arrived.

"Are you okay, Case?" A wide-eyed and worried Lindsay asked as she grabbed my hand and looked me up and down. That's when I realized that some of my captor's bits and pieces had found their way onto me, and I was quite a sight. Not surprising, as the larger caliber, sub-sonic round that had been used on him had made quite a mess.

"I'm good, but you should see the other guy. On second thought, you really shouldn't." I gave her a quick reassuring hug before Murph handed me a much needed Chuck's martini on the rocks. I noticed the bad case of the shakes I had earlier had now subsided almost completely.

Dawn sat with me on the couch as Rikki came in. I could see she had news.

"The Golden Gal strip club just exploded. That girl Crystal is dead, Tony Pro's car is in the parking lot but there's no sign of him, and Jimmy just took off. Looks like Paulie Attanasio decided to clean house in VA Beach. Two guys were watching from across the street in a car with New Jersey plates. They drove off right after it happened, but before Jimmy did. I'd say that the VA Beach underworld might be under new local management by tomorrow."

I raised my vodka, "Here's to that! I have no idea what I did to make that man come after me like he did, but I'm damn sure glad the shoe's now on the other foot."

18

CHANGES

J immy peeled out from in front of what was left of his business, preparing to implement his escape plan. You didn't live as long as he had being in bed with the mob without staying a step or two ahead of things. Having a very good escape plan for when it all goes south was also key. Hopefully, it would take a while before Paulie discovered he didn't die in the explosion and fire.

Tonight he had gotten lucky, and Angela had paid his price for him. But the chances of him dodging a "second bullet" were next to nil if he didn't get moving. Eventually, Paulie would find out he had missed, and this time there would probably be an open contract out on him. It wouldn't be just some of Paulie's guys. Ironically, he knew that some of his own contractors would be the ones that would then be looking for him. Now time was of the essence. The longer Paulie thought he was dead, the farther away he could get, and the safer he'd be.

As much as he'd enjoyed the house on Bay Island, it wasn't worth dying for. But he wasn't going to abandon it, either. His lawyer had a Power of Attorney on file, with instructions on what to do once he received a coded email from a certain generic email account. The proceeds from the sale of all his assets would be wired to an existing offshore account. All he had to do was lay low for a month or two, then he could slip out of the country. He couldn't do that yet, as he knew they'd be watching for him.

There was the matter of that Shaw guy, too. Though with Angela now gone, the chances of that deal going through successfully or him getting to the cash if it did were also next to nil. Damn.

As soon as he reached the house he grabbed a sledgehammer and went into his huge, tile walk-in shower. He smashed the center of one of the tile and tileboard walls, revealing a hidden cache with a pair of large black nylon gym bags loaded with cash, weapons, and a full set of documents for three new identities, as well as several new burner phones. Grabbing both bags, he made his way to his boat.

After starting the engines, Jimmy didn't even wait for them to warm up before backing out of his slip. He figured there was about an hour and a half before dawn, and he had just under an hour's ride to the tiny one-man boatyard on a river up off of Mobjack Bay. The owner of the yard specialized in maintaining boats whose owners didn't like questions. He texted the man, hoping he would wake up and read it before Jimmy arrived.

Forty-five minutes later he pulled up to the ways, a device similar to a large boat trailer mounted on rails that extend down into the water. The yard owner had gotten the message, and the cradle was waiting down in the water. A couple of low lights were on in the shed up where the boat would be pulled into. No greetings were exchanged, as the owner and Jimmy went about the business of hauling his boat as quietly as possible. Noise travels fast and far over water, and they both wanted to avoid detection.

If all goes as planned, a little over forty-eight hours from now *Polecat* will re-emerge from the shed as *Happy Hour II*, with a dark blue hull. Two years ago Jimmy had bought an identical hurricane-wrecked boat by that name. He had kept the registration active for this very reason, even though he had scrapped what was left of that boat. This job would put a dent in his cash, but it was all figured into his plan. Secrecy doesn't come cheap, but right now it was the only security he had.

~

I MANAGED A THREE-HOUR NAP. Frankly, I could've slept for a week, but there was work to be done. I called Larry Markham and got him to look up Joey's attorney's cell number from the information he gave the town. Despite it being a bit before his normal work hours, he picked up on the second ring, and he didn't sound happy about it. I didn't care.

"This is Casey Shaw."

"My client is dead, Mr. Shaw. We have nothing further to discuss."

"Your *real* client is alive and I need to get a message to him."

"I have no idea what you're talking about."

I said, "Humor me for a second, let's just say that you *do* know. If you do, your client would be very interested in hearing what you might tell him."

There was a pregnant pause before he said, "What might that be?"

"He missed the 'Eye' last night. And every minute that goes by until he finds that out, the trail keeps getting colder."

Again a pause as he thought about the information. "Why would you care, Shaw, what would you get out of telling me this?"

"I might have a vested interest in seeing what got started, gets finished. And I have no beef with your client, I only want to be left alone. That other party didn't see it that way."

This time there was no hesitation. "I'll call you back." After he hung up his regular cell phone the lawyer turned on a burner phone and dialed.

"WHAT? ARE YOU SURE ABOUT DAT?" Paulie is not the kind of guy who likes surprises or bad information.

"I made some calls, and Shaw's right. Not only that, but Jimmy was out the money for the hit on Shaw, so he grabbed him to try and squeeze it out of him. There was a fire in one of Jimmy's stash houses, and they found a body. I'm thinking it didn't go so well for one of Jimmy's guys, since Shaw's out running around."

"What's Shaw want out of this?"

"For you to catch up with Jimmy. And for Shaw to be left alone. He said he's got no beef with you."

"This Shaw guy, he's got some brass balls, I gotta give him that. But I got no beef with him, either. And we need things to settle down around there so we can get back to business as usual. Anything happens to Shaw, it'll make big news, an' that's the last thing we need down there right now. That'll just keep the Feds all worked up. We'll make sure the word gets out that nobody touches Shaw."

"Understood. Do I tell Shaw that?"

"Yeah."

PAULIE CALLED HIS LIEUTENANT. "You missed Jimmy, an' now he's inna wind. Find his ass and don't miss again. Get help wit' it, anybody you need, I want Jimmy. An' any contract he mighta had out on Shaw is canceled. You make sure everybody down there knows dat."

"Got it, Paulie."

MY PHONE RANG, it was the attorney calling back. A lot of how I might be living my life for the foreseeable future hung on what he had to say.

"Mr. Shaw, my client said he sees no conflict between you two. In fact, he believes that will continue to be the case in the future, and he is certain that his associates will all feel the same way. I hope I'm making myself clear on this point."

I hoped my sigh of relief wasn't audible across the phone. "You are. I appreciate you making the call."

"Your information was appreciated. Goodbye, Mr. Shaw." The phone went dead.

I looked across the dining table and smiled at Dawn, who had also been holding her breath to see what the news would be.

"No problems, and that's with him as well as his 'associates,' so I'm taking that to mean we're covered."

Dawn asked, "What if he's lying?"

"I'd be worried if we had the rail yard property in hand and the Chief was trying to shop a deal. But with him gone, Attanasio doesn't have any interest in that dirt. Trust me though, I'm still not going to be dropping my guard anytime soon, and neither should you."

I looked directly into Dawn's eyes. "This was the second time in a month that I thought I might never see you again. I know you want a church wedding up at your parent's, but I don't want to wait."

"We covered all the legal stuff, Case."

"Not quite. We covered everything that gives you all the authority that my wife would have. But I want the part about being able to introduce you as my wife, too. Let's go ahead and get married. We'll still do the whole church thing this fall, but I want to do this now. If you do."

Dawn nodded at me. I saw she had started to tear up, and I guess she didn't trust her voice right then. As badass as she is, it's nice to see she can still be at a loss for words every now and then. These last two days had really taken a toll on her. When she regained her composure, she said, "I hate to ask, but who's going to be your best man?"

"There's only one person who's been my friend the longest. But I understand if you don't want him there, and I'll pick someone else."

She gave me a rueful smile. "He hurt me more than I've ever been hurt by anyone before. But when I got that call yesterday I realized I needed Lindsay here, but I called Murph. I knew then I needed him here with me, too. Somehow I felt stronger by having him here, and don't you ever tell him I said that! But, no, I can't think of anybody else who should be standing there with you. Especially since I'm going to have Lindsay stand up for me." She paused for a minute, "I think we should break it to my dad gently, maybe much closer to the church wedding? In fact, let's not tell my parents about this one at all."

I laughed.

She said, "What?"

"He'll hate the idea of Murph in the wedding even more than the idea of you marrying an old fart like me, so maybe it'll take some of the heat off!"

She started chuckling, then it turned into laughter as she pictured me breaking the news and explaining my choice to her father.

I said, "I have an idea. Captain Frank is a Notary Public, and that means he can perform weddings. Let's take *Lady Dawn* out and get Frank to marry us."

"I love it, let's ask him," Dawn replied. Then she stared off into space for a few seconds before focusing on me again. "I've been thinking..."

"Nothing good ever comes from that," I quipped.

"Very funny. Our new slip will be ready tomorrow, right? The inlet will be open and clear?"

I nodded.

Then she said, "What would you think about leaving from here, but then tying up over there when we come back? Kind of a whole 'new beginning' thing. We could take some of the gang with us, make it a cruise and party. Sandy, Micah, Baloney, Betty, Kari, Marlin, Rikki, Cindy, Eric, Candi, and Missy."

Betty is Baloney's much better half, Candi Ryan is Eric's girlfriend and "Missy" is his teenage daughter. This would be a great group. "You're sure you don't want to invite your parents?"

"The church wedding is all mom's, and there's no sense in telling her that it came second. And I don't want to tell her anything about your being kidnapped. Besides, it'll take you more than two days to hide after you break the Murph news to my dad."

"Yeah, thanks for that."

"Hey, he's your pal!"

"Who came running to your rescue when you needed him." I paused then added, "I'm glad he did, and that you called him. There's been a lot of water past the stern since all that... stuff... happened.

Like you said, this is a whole 'new beginning,' and not just for you and me."

Dawn nodded. "Well, we've got a lot to do today to get this all put together. You go find Frank, and I'll start making calls."

Frank was honored to be asked to officiate and said he would gather all the paperwork. Chef Shauna was just as happy to have a big group to cook for. As I've said before, crews don't like to sit at the dock all the time. This short cruise should be fun for them as well, even if they do have to pull it all together in the next thirty hours. Plus, our crew is part of our family, and while technically they're going to be working, I wanted them all to be present for the ceremony.

We asked Linds and Murph to stop by since we wanted to ask them in person. Both were ecstatic and accepted. Then Dawn and Linds were off in their own world of planning. I looked at Murph and nodded my head toward the door. I don't think the women even noticed when we left.

We made our way over to C2 to check on the progress, and to get the heck off the boat while all the planning was going on. The docks were now all secured, with water, electric, and pump-out lines in place and operational. The last of that wooden freighter was being crushed and loaded onto a materials barge with a large excavator. The parking area was now paved, and the prefabbed metal roof over the parking places would be finished by tonight.

"You've always moved fast, Case, but I think this is a new record."

"It helps that we've given all these contractors a lot of business, and they know there's a bunch of work ahead, too. It cost me a few favors, but they understood why I'm in a big hurry to get over here. They read the paper, too."

We walked over to the boathouse where it was in the final stages of being re-sided, reroofed, and electrified. Inside, Murph was amazed.

"These lights make it look a lot larger inside."

He was right, and now with new floating docks down each side, recycled plastic decking materials on the stationary rear dock, and the bright lighting, it no longer resembled the place where I had almost met my end. I'm glad that it wouldn't be a constant reminder to me of that day. I'm looking forward to getting *Incognito* inside, and out of the elements.

Our next stop was the C2 clubhouse part of the *Cove Club*. It would mostly match what we had built over at *Bayside*, with a steam room, sauna, bar, large screen TV, and a pool table. But there were more rooms in the building, and that was visible now that the slab was in place and walls had started going up.

"What's this other part, Case?"

"A one-room apartment. Temporary quarters for when the boat is hauled out for maintenance or being repositioned for a trip or tournament."

"Nice. Good thinking, too."

I said, "We had the experience of the old club facility to draw on. See how the pool is twenty-percent larger, as is the deck since we'll have more of us using it. The outdoor kitchen is going to be roofed this time, too. You live and learn." That's when the irony of that statement hit me. I almost hadn't lived to see this. Twice.

Looking out from the new clubhouse across the pool, at first the view doesn't appear as stunning as the one at Bayside, which was out over the wide bay out toward the commercial channel. This view, however, was much more interesting. All the way to the left was the new helicopter and seaplane ramp. A little to the right and beyond the marsh grassed jetty was the Virginia Inside Passage. The grassy marsh lined and protected the other side of the channel. From C2 we had a great view across that channel and over the marsh and to Smith Island beyond. To the left was the decommissioned Cape Charles lighthouse on Smith Island. More to the right was Fisherman Island, and the first two spans of the CBBT. At night from here you can see the lights of VA Beach and an orange glow from Hampton. A little more to the right is our boat basin. Any view of Mallard Cove is completely blocked by that thirty yard deep woods which parallels their eastern property line. Of course, that works both ways. When we cut through the fence and installed the electric gate, we angled and curved the driveway to prevent any view beyond those trees to maintain our privacy over here.

Murph and I continued out beyond the new *C2* over to where the seaplane ramp and helicopter pad had been poured. A painter was busy painting a large "H" within a circle on the flat slab. The concrete extended farther north where a hanger would eventually sit.

"You're going to get a helicopter?"

"You never know, Murph. If I do, I'll have a place to keep it. In the meantime, I'm sure Eric will get some use out of it, starting tomorrow. There's no time like the present to get as much construction done as possible, before all the boats get in here. I'm assuming you don't want a bunch of construction dust and dirt blowing around and getting ground into your decks after you move in."

"Good thinking because no, I don't. Hey, how soon before the pool will be swimmable?"

I said, "Couple of weeks. All the exterior construction should be done by then. The whole project should be wrapped up by the end of the month, barring any unforeseen issues."

"Don't ever say that again. This has been a hell of a month."

"Yeah, but that's all in the past now. I'm looking forward to a very boring rest of the year."

"Aren't we all," Murph commented.

BY THE END of the afternoon, everything above *Polecat's* rub rail was cocooned in plastic or paper. Jimmy had been helping the boatyard owner mask and prep the boat. It was either this or he would have had to bring in one of his part-time helpers, which Jimmy vetoed because of security concerns. The boatyard owner, who he only knew as "Max," had a reputation for being discreet and reliable. But the fewer people who knew about the changes to his boat, the better. By nightfall the hull had been sanded, and tomorrow it would get several coats of blue sprayed onto it. *Polecat* was now only a memory.

Very soon, Jimmy would be changing his appearance as well. He planned on shaving his head and using a self-tanner on his skull as soon as he got the boat out of here. He had already stopped shaving his beard and would make a point of getting out more in the sun, letting nature take over the tanning part of his disguise.

After leaving the boatyard the day after tomorrow, he planned to continue living on the boat. He was going to make his way up the eastern side of ESVA, taking the Virginia Inside Passage channel and anchoring in the many bays along the way. He wanted to take his time and reach Wachapreague in about ten days, when he could top off his fuel and water tanks. He would then continue north to the Chesapeake and Delaware Canal where he'd head west for the Chesapeake Bay again, this time turning south to Baltimore where he'd leave the boat with a brokerage. By that time things should have cooled off enough for him to catch a flight to somewhere warm, and build a new life with a new name.

The beauty of his plan was that nobody would ever expect him to head farther up into territory that Paulie controlled. The trick was to stay out of the more populous areas. Smaller populations meant little or no business opportunities for Paulie's organization, so nobody nearby should recognize Jimmy as he made his way north.

Happy Hour II was a boat that for years had a rich fishing history down in North Carolina, much of it documented online in photographs. The now ex-*Polecat* will not only sport that new name, but the North Carolina hailing port as well. Anyone who bothered to check it would find the boat model and hull color matches the online history. They'd also find the pictures of the wrecked boat, and an article from two years ago stating how the new, unnamed owner planned on restoring the boat to her former greatness. He was covered. Now for the color change.

19

HAPPY HOUR

The next day I woke up and looked over at Dawn lying in bed next to me. As usual, she was already awake and watching me.

"It's bad luck to see the bride on your wedding day," she said.

I replied, "That's a misquote. It should be, 'It's bad luck if you don't see *all* of your bride on the morning of your wedding.'"

She grinned, "It is, eh? I thought that was supposed to come later?"

"Never put off for later what you can also do now," I replied with a smile.

FORTY-FIVE MINUTES later we went upstairs to find Murph and Lindsay having breakfast at our galley table. Evidently today we would each have a companion to keep us on track, and feeding them had become part of the deal.

"It's about time you two got up. We have things to do Dawn. And Casey, you weren't supposed to see your bride today," Lindsay scolded.

"Too late. Several other things aren't supposed to happen before the wedding either, but I think we worked our way down that list, breaking all of them as well," Dawn replied. "And that was just this morning."

Murph almost blew coffee out of his nose, laughing. "Hey, speaking of that, I forgot to put together a bachelor party for you last night. Maybe you and I can go to a strip club around lunchtime, Case."

Dawn scowled at him, "Or, not! I'd rather have a glitter-free and sober groom at my wedding, thank you very much."

I added, "No strippers, I've had bad luck around them lately." I guess the fact that I can joke about this is a good sign after what I went through. And I never quite understood the whole using "glitter as a cosmetic" for strippers. Why not just have a stamp for guys' foreheads instead that reads, "*I've Been To Flashdance!*"

Lindsay added, "And if you want to keep working down that list ourselves babe, you had better steer clear of strip clubs, too. If I ever see any glitter on you, anywhere..."

Murph held up his hand, "Got it. I'll be living a glitter-less life from now on."

"Wow, you're reforming the man, hats off to you! That, or he's just getting old," I said.

Murph retorted, "Hey! I'm still younger than you."

"Un huh, yet you're the second most senior person at this table right now. And now you're too old for strippers." I was having fun with this.

"I just told him to steer clear of strip clubs. He still has his own private stripper, and that's me. But I'm the one and only!" Lindsay leaned over and kissed him.

"Ugh, not before I've had breakfast you two, you'll wreck my appetite."

The fact that Dawn could joke about *this* confirmed how far she had come after what Murph put *her* through. I was thankful that she was now long past the uncomfortable stage, and that she was okay with Murph standing up for me tonight.

. . .

AFTER BREAKFAST, Murph and I cleared out, not wanting to be in the way as the crew decorated *Lady Dawn*, and Shauna prepared a huge seafood buffet for after the ceremony. Murph and I went to the Lynnhaven project since he hadn't been there in quite a while. It turned out to be great timing, as they were just about to break the earthen dam between Long Creek and the now completed basin.

We spotted Kari out by the dam and joined her as two long-armed excavators began digging as far as they could reach. After a couple of scoops, water began pouring into the basin, taking yard after cubic yard of earth along with it. A cameraman was recording the action and the video would be added to the project's website by this evening. We watched as the flow increased, the stream finally reaching the rear bulkhead as the excavators continued to deepen the breach.

Kari said, "They'll get the last of the material out of the center with that barge after the water level equalizes and the current stops. But by the time you say, "I do," tonight, you'll be able to take the *Lady Dawn* up in here."

Murph said, "Case, this is so far from the days back when you bought those old buildings and we rehabbed 'em. Glad I'm here to see this. Remind me to thank Dawn again for letting me back into your lives."

I laughed, "Two years ago if I had told her I wanted you to be my best man, I think she'd have broken our engagement. That's part of why I know I'm marrying the right woman this time; she knows how to forgive things."

"Forgive and forget," Murph said.

I replied, "Don't push it, while she's willing to forgive things, she never totally forgets."

Kari laughed, and I joined in as I saw Murph looked slightly chagrined.

We hung around another few minutes until the water level in the basin finally reached equilibrium with Long Creek. I had wanted to see the basin full, and now that it was, I told Kari we'd see her later on the boat and we left. But instead of heading to the tackle shop which was supposed to be next on our list, I pulled up an address on my smartphone. I entered it into the map app, and we turned onto the small bridge over Long Creek, and onto Bay Island.

Murph said, "I'm probably going to hate the answer to this, but where are we going?"

I smiled. "I figured that since we were this close, we ought to stop in on our old friend Jimmy."

"I was right. Have you lost your freaking mind?"

"Relax, Murph. No way he'll be there, but I'm curious."

"Yeah, there's a saying about that and cats, you know."

"I'm more of a dog person."

"Still, Case..."

"One quick look, then we're off to the tackle store, I swear."

THE GATES to the driveway leading out to Jimmy's house were closed, and there was crime scene tape across them. It was a straight shot down the driveway to the front door. Even from a hundred yards away we could see the police seals across the jamb and the door itself. Either something happened here to Jimmy, which we probably would have heard about, or the police had discovered evidence of some kind.

Much closer was the dock and its empty parking area. *Wet Dream* was still high and dry on its lift, but *Polecat*'s slip was empty, her dock lines trailing off into the water. Either someone unknowledgeable about boats had taken her from here, or whoever it was left in a big hurry. You always hang your dock lines from the pilings or leave them on the dock, high and dry. Leaving them in the water is a great way for them to get tangled on pilings, covered in slime, or sucked into a prop when you return. Or all three. I suspected we just discovered how Jimmy got away, and that he left in a big hurry. Couldn't blame him for that, I wouldn't want Attanasio after me, either. I told Murph what I thought.

"Great work, Sherlock Holmes. Can we go to the tackle store now?"

"Nervous?"

"Just cautious. You know, like you should be? Let's get out of here!"

MY OLD PAL Mark was working at the tackle store today. I didn't know what kind of welcome to expect since I knew he fished all around on lower ESVA, and no doubt he had heard about my arrest. But it turned out that he also heard about me being cleared, and was one of the people who cared about that part. I saw a huge smile on his heavily bearded face.

"Hey, welcome jailbird! I heard you broke out."

"The only thing 'breaking out' are the hives my wallet gets when I come in here," I retorted.

"Speaking of that, did you get it back from the cops? You know, the one Skeezix here gaffed?"

Murph said indignantly, "It wasn't a gaff, it was a 7/0 Mustad hook, and I was trying like heck to catch a citation sized bull mahi!"

"Instead you caught a 6 foot Casey." Mark roared at his own joke. "Well, did you just come in here for the free abuse? If you don't buy something, I'll have to start charging y'all for it."

"Between the two of us, we've already bought everything in here twice," Murph grumped.

I said, "Actually, I did come in here to buy something. Again. I bought a center console and I need a few rods and gear for it. I don't want to have to grab some off *Predator* every time I want to go, and I know my fian...er...*wife* will have already liberated them when I want to go fishing myself."

"Wife? You and Dawn finally tied the knot? Congratulations!"

Murph jumped in, "About six hours from now. I'm Casey-sitting to make sure he doesn't get cold feet."

I said, "I'm not going to get cold feet. You're the one who did that."

Murph said, "And if I hadn't, you wouldn't be getting married to her today, now would you?"

"Wait, were you and Dawn..." Mark looked confused.

"Yeah, yeah, bad story with a good ending. You want to show us rods or what, fur face?" Murph asked.

Mark shook his head as he led us over to the rods. I picked out several spinning rods in multiple weights, and four in twenty-pound and another four in thirty-pound with conventional gold anodized reels. After they were all filled with line, I picked out a couple of gaffs to go with them, and we loaded everything in my Jeep.

On the way to our next stop, fortunately Lindsay called Murph, because I needed some privacy. He stayed in the car to talk to her while I ran into the jewelry store to pick up the plain wedding band that went with Dawn's engagement ring. But I was also able to pick up two white marlin gold pendants and chains for Linds and Murph for standing up for us tonight. Then our last stop was for some fast food at a drive-through, before we headed back to the *Cove*. We drove through rain on the first span of the CBBT, and that's supposed to be lucky on your wedding day. I didn't tell Murph why I was smiling.

JIMMY WATCHED as Max applied coat after coat of polyurethane paint to the hull. They hadn't used primer since that added step would have consumed two more days, and Jimmy didn't care so much about quality as much as coverage and speed. He needed to get *Happy Hour II* back in the water, ASAP. Even without primer, Max's work was as good or better than many of the more modern boatyards that were equipped with elaborate ventilation systems. The finish was coming out like glass. And as hot as it is in the shed, the paint would dry and harden up quickly. They would apply the pre-cut vinyl lettering on the bow and the stern in the morning then "splash" the renamed boat and get Jimmy on his way.

While the heat in the shed was great for the paint, it wasn't good for Jimmy. With the boat out of the water, he couldn't use the air conditioner, which was a water-cooled unit. The temperature in the shed never dropped below eighty-five last night, and Jimmy tossed and turned. After somehow managing to grab two hours of sleep right before daybreak, he woke up covered in sweat on one of the bridge couches. As hot as that had been on the bridge, it was over ninety in the cabin. And those two hours of sleep had been all he had gotten in as many days. He hoped that the temperature would at least fall below eighty tonight, though it wasn't forecast to.

Max had loaned him a crappy respirator mask so that he could watch, but the damn thing leaked like a sieve. The chemicals in the polyurethane were getting him as stoned as he'd been in a while. This, combined with his lack of sleep was making him loopy. Max saw this and ordered him out of the shed while he finished the last coat. Once outside, he sat down on the base of the boatyard's old wooden dock, breathing in fresh air and regaining some of his senses.

He ran his timeline through his head again. Apply the new name in the morning, then a quick run down to Mobjack Bay. He doubted he'd have much better luck sleeping tonight, so he'd chill the cabin down and catch a few good hours of sleep. He wanted to be back moving by noon, and well beyond the high traffic Chesapeake.

His objective tomorrow was to get anchored in Magothy Bay. Very little traffic on that side of ESVA and people kept their noses to themselves. Only one thing was bugging him, he'd be passing Mallard Cove where that Shaw guy and his broad lived on their sportfish. What was it Tony said was the name? Right, it's *Predator*. Sounded like the guy was a short-eyed pedophile. He wished he'd never heard the son of bitch's name. His cousin and Angela would still be alive, he'd still have his business, he'd still have his *life*. Somehow, someday, he'd get even with that one.

WE STASHED the rods and gaffs in the salon on *Predator*. I wanted them as a wedding surprise for Dawn, to show her I was serious about sharing the boat.

Murph and I each grabbed a beer, and relaxed in the salon while looking over each new rod closely. I didn't expect to find any flaws since they were all custom made by the tackle shop's resident rod wrapper, but it was still good to check. Okay, having a beer and keeping myself busy by checking the rods, I'll admit that maybe I was getting a little nervous. After all, my last two marriages had cost me millions of dollars and chunks of my heart. Kind of hard to get totally past that...

"Hey CASEY!"

I guess Murph had been trying to get my attention for a bit. "What!"

He grinned, and said in a somewhat lower voice, "It's okay, pal, you made the right choice. This time."

"Yet you thought you had, too."

He looked surprised at my statement. I hadn't meant to say that, it just came out. I guess I'm more nervous than I thought.

Murph turned sideways on the couch to face me directly, his back to the door. "We've never really talked about this before Case, and from what you just said I think we ought to. I know at the time it happened, you probably figured I cheated on Dawn because I wasn't ready to give up my old ways."

I nodded. "Pretty much, Murph."

He sighed. "If that's what I had been doing, then why did I work so hard to get Lindsay back? Why in two years has there only been Lindsay? Don't bring up that French bitch. That wasn't me, it was all her, and I turned her down."

The French woman was part of another story from another day, but what he was saying was true. There had only been Lindsay for him after Dawn.

"No Case, a big part of the reason was that even though we were engaged, Dawn would sneak glances at you in a way she never even looked at me, and it hit me that she never would. She didn't do it on purpose, and I don't think she even realized when she was doing it.

"Maybe I didn't know how to break it off properly. Before her, long relationships were never my strong suit. She taught me a lot; I'm truly grateful for that, and you don't know how much I regret ever having hurt her. Though I know it would have been much worse if it happened later, and that was sure to be in the cards. You guys were meant to be together, not her and me.

"Then again, when I met Linds I felt something, and I guess I knew what it could turn out to be. That she could end up looking at me that same way Dawn glanced at you back then. And I was right, because she does."

"Michael Murphy, that is the sweetest thing you have ever said." Lindsay had quietly come through the door with Dawn, and both were standing behind Murph, having heard everything he said.

Yes, I could have given him a "heads up," but I didn't, and I'm glad. Lindsay hugged him from behind as I looked up at Dawn. I saw her start to tear up again. She reached beyond Lindsay and put a hand on Murph's shoulder. He looked up startled, then put a hand over hers and smiled.

I gave it a beat or two then said, "As long as everybody is getting so freaking mushy, look honey, I love you thiiiis much!" I gave her my best Carol Merrill from "*Let's Make A Deal*" impression, indicating the rods and gaffs with both hands.

"Casey, you can go fishing later. Hello, we have our wedding?"

"Ah, but what's a wedding without presents! For you, for *Incognito*."

The realization spread across her face as she first started beaming then came over and hugged me. Any nerves I had been feeling melted away right then. I was marrying a woman who appreciated rods and reels as a wedding gift. I had finally chosen well this time. Very well.

Jeff came through the door and stopped mid-step, having expected the boat to be empty. Instead, he saw Lindsay now straddling Murph's lap, and Dawn kissing me. The embarrassed look on his face was priceless.

I laughed and said, "Come on in, Jeff. Hey, if you're ever at a loss for what to get Micah as a present, go with fishing rods. You won't believe the reaction you'll get." That's when he spotted the rods. I laughed again. "They're for *Incognito*. We'll hang them in the boat shed when we move it over there."

A confused but relieved Jeff said, "Gotcha, Casey. And speaking of moving over there, I figure on moving *Predator* over sometime tomorrow, if that's all right. And thank you both for letting Micah bring me along as her date tonight."

"Sure, anytime tomorrow is fine. And you're family, we wouldn't have it any other way." Not only was Jeff a great boatman and fisherman, but he was also a class act. I meant it, we wanted him there with the full crew from *Lady Dawn*.

Jeff continued on down below, and I passed Dawn the necklace I bought for her to give Linds. She sneaked a look and nodded. We handed the boxes over to a surprised Murph and Lindsay. Murph stared at his as Lindsay put hers on. I saw Murph's face cloud up.

"No billfish were killed in the making of that necklace, pal," I joked.

He looked up with a worried face, as he held the box back toward me. "I can't take this, Case. I appreciate it, but I can only do half the job. While I'm happy to stand up for you tonight, I've been thinking. It's not a good idea for me to come up to Easton for your real wedding. It would be too uncomfortable for me and for Dawn's parents, especially her dad. That wedding is really for them, and I'm not going to ruin it for all of you. So, If you want somebody else for tonight, I understand."

I pushed the box back to him. "I appreciate that, but I want you to have this. Whether or not you stand up again for me up there is your call."

He reluctantly took the box and said, "I think it's for the best that I don't. I hate getting all gussied up anyhow. I'm glad that you guys made tonight 'Chesapeake Casual.' That'll be nice and relaxed.

Besides, I hate seeing Baloney in a coat and tie, it reminds me too much of funerals." He smiled.

Dawn looked at him, "Murph, thanks for making that sacrifice. To tell you the truth, I was dreading telling my father almost as much as I'm happy that we can be friends and that Lindsay became my best friend. Funny how things work out, isn't it? Put that necklace on, I'd love to have you both wearing them tonight."

Murph looked relieved, and Linds helped him with the chain clasp. "Thanks, Dawn. For all of that, and for this."

20

THE MORNING AFTER

I picked up Eric, Candi, and Missy over at the new pad as they landed. Kari had surprised me by having my "Caseymobile" brought down from Bayside. It's a jacked-up six-seater golf cart with knobby tires and a suspension that will allow it to go everywhere on the new property. We all loaded up as Eric remarked, "You've taken this place to a new level. I'm just sorry about what happened to make it come about, Casey."

"I'm not. Eric, it seems like things happen for a reason around the two of us. And you know, I think I've taken Bayside about as far as I can. With you building the biggest house out on the point, and your connections in our prime customer area, we'll be better off. You and Candi have become the new faces of *Bayside* and you're both already so well known. That'll give it a big boost while my new place allows me to get back to the privacy that I've been wanting and missing. But enough about business, we're all going to relax and enjoy tonight."

AS CAPTAIN FRANK pulled us away from the dock an hour before sunset, I was ready for what was ahead. Not just marrying Dawn, but also moving next door, as well as figuring out a new business role for myself. As I looked around at all my friends here on the flybridge & entertainment deck on top of *Lady Dawn*, I was truly happy. I saw Rikki, she smiled at me and I returned it. I owed her so much, because without her having rescued me from that warehouse, I'd have been left at the hands of that cokehead. There's no doubt he would have murdered me when his ride never showed back up and his paranoia increased. I needed to talk to her later tonight.

Frank took us into the Chesapeake, then turned us with our stern toward the sunset and let us drift so the whole crew could join us. They had launched my Maverick flats skiff earlier and removed its cradle from this upper deck to create more deck room for tonight. It normally sits up here all the way aft, beyond the hot tub, the large bar, and the "U" shaped booth and dinner table. Lindsay had arranged for a pair of musicians to set the mood, and a photographer to record the event.

Dawn looked incredible in a knee-length simple white dress with a matching white flower above her ear, island-style, while I was in chinos, an oxford, and my deck shoes. The photos with the water and the sunset behind us came out incredible. I don't know what I ever did to deserve this and Dawn too, but I'm so grateful to be here right now.

After the ceremony, Frank got us moving again while the sun finished setting off our stern. The crew had rigged a long string of white party lights overhead which lit the aft deck turning it into a dance floor. Baloney got a surprise when Sandy tapped him on the shoulder and cut in on him with Betty. It turned out that Sandy is quite a dancer. Baloney scowled from the sidelines where I was also taking a break.

"First the guy is always stealing my beer, then he steals my wife for a dance," he grumped.

"Don't you mean my beer, Bill?" I asked.

"What's the difference?"

The music ended, and Baloney went to reclaim his wife, but not before first getting a fresh bottle of Red Stripe. Life was back to normal.

"C'mon, you. Your wife is out there dancing, now it's my turn," Rikki grabbed my hand, pulling me out onto our impromptu dance floor next to where Dawn was dancing with Eric. Dancing has never really been my thing but hey, I'm among friends, not strangers. After the song stopped, I led Rik over to the side.

"You know that Murph is my oldest friend, Rik, but I've grown just as close to you over the past couple of years."

She grinned, "You're wasting your time pal, I'm taken, and so are you."

"Funny lady. You're one of the few who know the full story of him and Dawn."

She suddenly looked serious, "You know I do, and that I'll never say anything to anyone about it." One of those stories for another day.

I said, "He's not going up to our wedding this fall in Easton, it wouldn't be a good idea since her father, well..."

"Trust me, I get it."

"Well, I was wondering if you'd be willing to stand up as my "best person" that day."

It takes a lot to shock Rikki, and I just did. Her face softened and I suddenly found myself wrapped up in a bone-crunching hug.

"I take it that's a yes?"

She backed up a bit, still with one hand on either of my shoulders. "Of course it is, you idiot. I'd be honored. Tuxedos?"

I nodded, "Probably."

She grinned, "I think I can pull that off."

Dawn had walked up beside her, "Who are you kidding, you'd look majorly hot in a tuxedo! With your figure, you can rock most anything. Pardon us Case, I want to dance with our other "best person." She led Rikki back out on the floor.

"I'm going to miss you guys up at *Bayside*." Cindy had appeared at my side and put one arm through mine, not something she's prone to do, so I knew she meant it.

"Ah, just think of it as you now have a place to get away from it all, down at the new C2, anytime you want."

"Thanks, Case, but it's still not going to be the same."

"Nothing stays the same, Cin. Except my dancing, which still sucks. Want to get your toes mashed?"

"Hey, we can't let Dawn and Rik have all the fun, let's go!"

SHAUNA OUTDID herself with a seafood spectacular. Everything from lobster to sushi, sashimi, conch fritters, and fish chowder. Andrea was pouring booze and champagne non-stop from behind the bar. By the time we pulled into the new dock a little after midnight, everyone was full, and no-one was feeling any pain.

Eric's pilot had already taken the chopper back to *Bayside* since noise restrictions would have prevented him landing there this late. Instead, there was a car and driver waiting to take the three of them safely back. Baloney, Betty, Murph, Linds, Kari, Marlin and Sandy were all just a chip shot from their boats, and all managed to stagger home. Micah and Jeff were staying on *Predator*, and Rikki and Cindy had our VIP stateroom up forward on *Lady Dawn* for the night. We wanted everyone safe and accounted for.

I mixed four "Chuck's Martini's" on the rocks, and Dawn, Rikki, Cindy, and I sat on the aft deck. I held my glass aloft and declared, "Best wedding I ever had!"

As I expected, I got slugged in the shoulder by Dawn as I chuckled, but what I hadn't expected was a shot on the other arm by Rik, who said, "You are such an ass!" Then she joined in laughing.

"Yeah, well, it took you three tries to achieve perfection, pal, so now you can quit while you're ahead," said Dawn.

"Roger that, Mrs. Shaw."

"Mrs. Shaw. You know, I like the sound of that, especially coming from my husband. My one and only husband, since I got it right on the first try."

I was about to rib her about Murph, but the look Rik shot me changed my mind. You spend enough time fishing with someone and they can finish your sentences, or even stop you before you start one.

"Okay, Mrs. Shaw, shall we retire for the evening?"

"I still have half a drink left."

"Down it," I encouraged.

Rik said, "Hey if you two don't mind, we may take a hot tub up on the entertainment deck before we turn in."

Dawn put the now finished drink down. "Have at. Got all the privacy you need over here too, if you know what I mean." She looked at me, "C'mon old man, speaking of privacy..."

I didn't need to be asked twice.

THE NIGHT HAD BEEN JUST as hot as Jimmy had feared, and again it was mostly sleepless. Thankfully Max showed up an hour before daylight, and by dawn, the newly named *Happy Hour II* was sliding down the ways into the river. Jimmy cranked the generator and the air conditioner on the way over to Mobjack Bay. He anchored up, grabbed a quick shower, and hit the vee berth in cool comfort. His phone alarm went off right at ten a.m., though he had been asleep less than four hours. While he felt more refreshed than he had in days, he knew he still wasn't quite "firing on all cylinders."

He made a sandwich and pulled a bottle of water out of the 'fridge before cranking the engines, raising the anchor, and getting underway. He wanted to be anchored in Magothy Bay in the early afternoon so he could get some real sleep.

The hour-long trip across the bay was smooth, and the synchronized harmonic resonance of the engines lulled him into kind of a stupor along the way. He shook it off as he reached the southern point of ESVA and passed under Fisherman Inlet Bridge. Just ahead on the left were the buildings of *Mallard Cove* and the beach where a few of the rental catamarans were still available today.

A large sportfish was coming out of the marina ahead, taking a hard left in into the VA Inside Passage. But instead of speeding up, it stayed at a fast idle, forcing Jimmy to back down off a plane to avoid running up on it, even though it was still a hundred or so yards in front of him. It started turning hard to port into a narrow inlet, just as

Jimmy recognized the name on the transom. *Predator.* There was a man and a woman on the bridge, obviously Shaw and his girlfriend. Reacting out of hatred and without any thought, Jimmy pulled out his pistol and began firing, and he saw both figures go down.

CASEY AWOKE AS USUAL, looking into Dawn's eyes. Only today, they were a tad bloodshot.

"Good morning, Mrs. Shaw."

"It has yet to be seen how good it is, Mr. Shaw."

"Well, it is the first day of our non-honeymoon, honeymoon." I raised one eyebrow.

"Mmmm, yes, it is, isn't it? But it's already after nine-thirty a.m., and we've wayyy overslept. We're late for breakfast."

"Hmm, well then, how about being early for lunch?"

WE MADE our way up to the salon deck an hour later, finding Rik and Cindy still having breakfast and looking as fuzzy as we felt.

"Good morning, kids!" Dawn was feeling better.

"Not so loud. Whose bright idea was it to have both champagne *and* vodka last night?" Cindy looked the worse for wear of all of us.

"If I recall correctly, it was your 'significant other' that was feeding you drinks, so don't blame me," I said.

Rikki retorted, "You were the one pushing the 'Chuck's' last night!"

I said, "Well, it's good stuff."

She agreed, "It is, and champagne always gives me a headache anyway."

I winked at Cindy, "Sorry."

She grinned, "At least headaches were this morning, not last night in the hot tub, which is amazing, by the way."

Shauna came in, bringing coffee for Dawn and me. Dawn looked grateful, "Ah, an angel of mercy. Thank you, Shauna! By the way, last night's dinner was fantastic! Where did you learn to make wedding cakes?"

"Learned that as a little girl, baking with my mom. And speaking of cakes, I have two piles of pancakes, coming right up!" She went back into the galley.

Rikki said, "If you are paying her less than the President of the USA's salary, you're not paying her enough."

"I heard that. She knows how to deal with the 'morning afters,'" Cindy said.

Dawn chuckled, "Unfortunately, we've given her some practice."

A PILE of pancakes and a gallon of coffee later, Andrea answered a knock at the dockside door. Special Agent Stephanie Baker came into the salon.

"Sorry to disturb you all this morning."

I said, "Not disturbing us, we're just getting a late start after our wedding last night."

She blinked, "Seriously? Well, congratulations. Again, I hate to interrupt, but could I talk to you outside, Mr. Shaw?"

I led her to the aft deck, getting my first daylight look at our view from the new slip. We had about twenty feet from the stern to the low, grass-covered jetty that formed one side of our little basin. I could see the water of the protected cut of the VA Inside Passage just beyond. Then about seventy-feet to the left was the break in the jetty where the freighter had once been.

"A few things have happened since we last talked. Jimmy Impasato's club down in VA Beach exploded and burned to the ground, taking two of his associates with it. We're certain they had help in getting sent to Valhalla."

Out of the corner of my eye I saw *Predator* approaching, with Jeff and Micah on the flybridge.

"Jimmy Impasato has vanished, and a property of his just north of here also burned on the same night, also taking another of his associates with it, and he had help, too. I'm just dotting 'I's' and crossing 'T's' here, would you happen to know anything about any of that?"

I was distracted as I had been watching a dark-blue-hulled express sportfisherman that was closing fast on *Predator* just as she started making the turn into her new home. There was something vaguely familiar about its shape. Some bald-headed guy was at the helm, and as I watched, he raised a pistol and started shooting at Jeff and Micah. I watched horrified, as I saw both go down.

"Nooooo!" Too late, I realized this was the same boat as the one at Jimmy's dock, but it had been painted a different color. I pulled my Glock and emptied all fifteen rounds out of the magazine. The boat sped up and disappeared down "the ditch" in seconds. I focused back on *Predator* and saw that Micah was now at the helm. I couldn't see Jeff. I could hear her screaming for help as she pointed my boat bow-in to its new slip.

"Put the gun down, Shaw."

I turned and stared down the barrel of Baker's Glock. I slowly set mine down on the table, hands raised. "I'm pretty certain that was Impasato who just shot at my crew on my other boat. That blue boat looks identical to his, except for the color."

We could hear Micah screaming for help, and I could see Baker weighing what I'd said. A second later she said, "Pick up your weapon, Shaw, and come on!"

Rik, Dawn, and Cindy all came racing out as Special Agent Baker and I went tearing down the side deck to the gangway. She was already calling for help on her cellphone. When we reached *Predator*, Jeff was sitting up on the flybridge deck, holding a bleeding upper arm. It was a "through and through," meaning the bullet wasn't lodged in his arm, and it wasn't life-threatening.

"Who was that, and why did he shoot at me?"

"The same guy who sent that last shooter. He probably thought you were me. I'm going to go put an end to this." I turned and started running next door to grab *Incognito* when I heard Agent Baker yell.

"Shaw! Stop!"

I stopped and turned, noticing her hand was on her now

holstered pistol. I said, "You can either stay here, or you can come with me and catch this guy."

"How?"

"My outboard. Are you coming or not?" Dawn, and Cindy were helping Jeff, and I wanted this guy now, more than ever. Rik was coming up the dock, heading straight for me. "Rikki, stay here and help Jeff."

"Like hell, I will! He'll be fine, Dawn and Cin can take care of him. I'm coming with you two, I've got my firearm with me."

I saw Baker nod at her, and the three of us double-timed it to my outboard. They were untying us as I cranked the engine. We shot out of the marina as I went wide-open-throttle with her, banking left down the cut. Our top speed was probably at least five knots above that of the blue boat, which was nowhere in sight. As we shot down "the ditch," Baker took a phone call while I took my spare magazine from my holster and reloaded.

After she hung up she said, "We'll have a chopper here from Quantico in twenty minutes."

We shot out of the cut into more open water. Magothy Bay was ahead on the left, and there was a marsh and scrub island to our right. There was no sign of the blue boat up the bay, but I knew it wasn't fast enough to have already gotten completely out of sight if it had gone that way. It had to have turned to the right, behind the scrub island. I started to do the same thing.

21

HIT THE BEACH

Jimmy had let his anger get the best of him. That, coupled with his lack of sleep had allowed him to make the worst mistake of his life, going after Shaw in broad daylight. He realized it too late after he pulled the trigger the first time. As soon as the man and the woman went down on the sportfisherman, he saw holes appearing in the bulkhead next to him. Suddenly he had a searing pain in his side, and then another in his back. He jammed the throttles wide open, ducking down as far as he could as more holes erupted in the bulkhead. His left side and back both felt like two red-hot pokers were sticking in them. He glanced back and on the stern of a yacht he saw a man with a pistol who had been the one shooting at him.

For a split second Jimmy thought about returning fire, but then the pain distracted him. Looking down, he saw the front left side of his shirt was already wet and red. He had to get away from the shooter and do something to stop the bleeding. He continued down the ditch and briefly considered running up Magothy Bay. But he decided that he needed to find a place to stash the boat fast, well out of sight of the channel so that he could deal with his wounds. So much for him keeping a low profile.

Once clear of the ditch he looked over the scrub island just beyond it to the right, but it was too small. As he passed by it, he spotted Smith Island Bay a little less than a mile away over to starboard. It looked like there was a large creek leading from it back up into the mudflats of Smith Island, and behind the scrub which would provide good cover. He turned toward the mouth of the bay, keeping the throttles on the pegs.

Weaving between the small sandbar islands as he approached, he was preoccupied with his wounds and the pain. He totally missed seeing the wire cages of the shellfish farm ahead in the water until he was right on top of them. Several of the cages got caught and twisted up into his propellers, slowing the boat and stalling the port engine. The starboard prop had so much wire wrapped around the blades that it now could barely push the boat.

With what little speed he could make, he aimed toward the muddy shore at the narrowest part of the island. He could see the backside of a sand dune maybe a hundred yards in. Jimmy knew there would be a long sandy beach along the Atlantic Ocean on the other side, and that the only way to reach it was by boat. Some families come here to picnic and if he got lucky, maybe there would be a boat over there now that he could steal and use to get away.

ONCE WE CLEARED the scrub island I saw something blue and white far up in Smith Island Bay, up near the shore, but it wasn't moving. I aimed for it, and as we got closer I saw that it was indeed the boat the shooter had been in. I also saw that it had gone right through a shellfish farm, and looked to be disabled. Baker called in an update and gave the boat's location.

From here it looked like the boat was deserted, but still we approached carefully. I slowed us down to idle and raised the engine enough to make it through the shallows beyond the shellfish farm. I put our bow against the stern of the blue boat and Baker stepped cautiously onboard. Quickly checking the cabin she came back out and said, "He's not here."

I looked down at the deck and saw all the blood. "Well, I don't think he's going to get far losing that much blood. He must be trying to get to the beach. Get back aboard, and I'll get us in as close as I can."

I raised the engine as high as I could without exposing the cooling water intakes. Then I went up another creek which brought us within fifty feet of the sand dune. I set the anchor in the mud in front of us as we slogged our way through the mud over to the dry sandy shore. Jimmy was nowhere in sight as we scrambled up over the low dune, guns in hand. But maybe two hundred yards down the beach along the dune edge were a couple of black nylon gym bags.

We made our way over to the bags, only to find a blood trail and a set of footprints. They led down from the dune past the bags and to the ocean. Baker checked the bags while Rik and I scanned the area. There was no sign of anyone in the water, but twenty yards or so away I spotted what I thought was another blood trail and set of footprints that led back up the dune. I turned and looked where the first set had originated and saw Jimmy cresting the top, gun drawn on us, he had doubled back.

Jimmy yelled, "Drop your guns! And give me the keys to your boat."

He looked pale and was swaying a little as he spoke, the lower third of his shirt bright red. But his gun stayed steady, pointed in our direction. I didn't drop my gun, but I put both hands up out in front of me, my barrel pointing upward. I moved over between Jimmy and Special Agent Baker, who was still bent over the bags. I was maybe five feet in front of her, and I hoped it would be enough cover.

I saw that Rik had done the same with her hands, also retaining her weapon, which pointed upward like mine. The problem was, Jimmy's aim was alternating back and forth between Rik and me, now that I was covering Baker. If Rik or I made a move to aim at him, I had no doubt in my mind that he'd be able to shoot one of us before we could get him in our sights.

Baker said barely above a whisper, "When I say drop, hit the deck." By being on one knee kneeling next to the bags, she was in a classic shooting position. Her left hand was out and up like ours and in full view of Jimmy. However, I had blocked Jimmy's view of her shooting arm, and she was pre-aimed, behind my back.

Baker watched as Jimmy started to swing his aim over to Rik, and she said, "Drop."

I dove for the sand and both felt the concussions and heard the three shots from behind me as the bullets passed close by my head. Too late, Jimmy had seen my movement and tried to re-acquire me as a target when all three of Baker's bullets found their marks. Jimmy tumbled backwards, this time he was dead before he hit the sand. Her first shot was a heart shot.

Rick ran up the dune, retrieved Jimmy's pistol, and checked for the non-existent pulse. She confirmed it saying simply, "He's dead."

Baker stood, and offered me a hand up. "You all right?"

"I'm not hit, if that's what you mean, but I'm gonna be deaf for a month."

She chuckled, "At least you'll still be around to be deaf."

"Yeah, there *is* that. Thank you, by the way."

"It's all part of the job."

"I meant for missing me!"

"That too," she laughed.

Off in the distance we heard a helicopter approaching. I watched as it circled and descended out over the ocean and landed fifty yards down the beach from us. I saw Baker get her game face on as several other FBI agents climbed out of the chopper. I knew her day was about to get a lot longer.

LATER IN THE day when Jeff got back from the hospital, I had him come into *Lady Dawn*'s salon since I owed him an apology.

"I'm really sorry that you got shot because of me. I had no idea Impasato was still around, or that he'd be after me."

Jeff was no stranger to the trouble I'd run into over the past few years.

"Wasn't your fault, Casey, you didn't pull the trigger."

"No, but if you hadn't been aboard *Predator*, he wouldn't have shot at you."

"You can't figure out what some whack job will do ahead of time."

"Hey, Jeff, not to change the subject, but do you think you can still crank on a billfish or two?"

"Sure, in a few days. It's not that bad a wound, it's just sore right now."

"I know we were talking about fishing the next Hatteras billfish tournament, but I don't think I'll be able to break away. Why don't you and Micah go fish it in *Predator*, and take a couple of friends with you. Take a week down there, I'll pay her too, and pay all the expenses for the trip and tournament."

"Casey, you don't have to do that!"

"But I want to. Just make sure you win the darn thing, we need to keep up our boat's reputation." I smiled when I saw how pleased Jeff was. The best fishing captains hate sitting around the dock. And I hated that he got hurt because of me. "Oh, and don't take my new rods with you! Dawn will have both our butts."

"I'll get them hung up in the boat shed before we go."

As he turned and left, Dawn came in.

"He like the tournament idea?"

"Loved it. I'm glad they'll have some fun. And now that Impasato's gone, we can as well."

"So the mob is out of the area now."

I shook my head. "Not likely. Just changed local management. When I was a kid in South Florida, boats and people used to disappear all the time. Every two-bit punk could grab a boat, make a grass run, then scuttle the boat. As things switched to coke and the stakes got higher, lives got cheaper. It didn't matter if there were people on the boats they stole, they were just inconveniences. It wasn't until the cartels and the mob stepped in and stopped the slaughter and theft that the water started being safe again. They're businesspeople, just without any sort of moral compass. They buy their transport boats and planes now instead of stealing them. Losing a certain percentage of these is figured into the overhead.

"But the mob doesn't want any disruptions such as FBI investigations. They only want a smooth money flow. Just because 'Jimmy the Eye' is dead, the demand for narcotics, hookers, and even hitmen hasn't waned. Someone is going to step into the vacuum he created by dying and fill it. Had he stuck to the plan instead of coming after me, he'd probably still be in charge. He got outside of the purview that was set for him by Attanasio, and that was his fatal mistake."

Dawn asked, "So now he owes you a favor?"

"I doubt very much that he would see it that way. No, I'm guessing he probably would call it even. And that's fine by me."

ANDREA SHOWED Special Agent Baker in a few minutes after I saw the FBI helicopter land on my new pad. Dawn and I were sitting on the aft deck. I stood and motioned to a chair next to where Dawn was sitting.

"I hear congratulations are in order, Mrs. Shaw."

"Thank you, and the same to you for closing your case."

"Yes, well, about that. Mr. Shaw, I have a few questions for you. It turns out there are some gaps in the story."

I said, "Shoot. That's a figure of speech, by the way. Oh, and talk loudly, I've got a lot of ringing in my ears this afternoon." I smiled at her.

"Right. Well, like I said, about those gaps. How did you know what Impasato's boat looked like?"

I told the story of "Sport" showing up and spying on Dawn and me. I told her how Murph said he stared at the bow of Predator, where the name is easily seen, and how we had followed him down to Impasato's house. I also said that nothing further had come of it, that I supposed he was trying to rattle me because Impasato must've blamed me for the death of his cousin. I didn't say anything about the kidnapping, or Crystal/Angela. I could tell Baker wasn't buying it.

"Special Agent Baker, here's the thing. I'm not one of the bad guys. I got sucked into this thing not of my own volition. My business is clean, and I have no ties to anyone in the mob. You can ask anyone about that. I'm going to develop the rail yards in Cape Charles, and you can check on my partners and our financing, everything is above board."

She stared at me for a few seconds. "I've already done that. I get the feeling that what you've told me is true, though I don't think you've told me the entire story. But I've got what I need to wrap this up, and I don't need any more paperwork than I've already got." She extended her hand, which I shook. Even though our business was concluded, I had a feeling it wouldn't be the last we'd see of her.

EPILOGUE

S*ix Weeks Later...*

IT WAS the first of what I hoped would be a lot of *C2* parties, and everyone was enjoying themselves. I looked out on our now full cove, home to most of our closest friends. Even the ones who didn't tie up here were present for the party, and it was a classic. Oh, and I had the best view at *C2* right now because I was on the second floor of a big two-story Seminole chickee tower I had my Seminole friend Noah Billie come up from Florida to build. You know how I love not needing to get a building permit for chickees.

Jeff, Micah, and their friends just returned from the Hatteras tournament after taking second place. His arm is completely healed, and he's happy that he was able to get "off the dock" and keep *Predator's* reputation intact.

Speaking of reputations, mine is back on the mend in Cape Charles where we've taken title to the rail yards. We should be breaking ground there in another couple of months. But even better, Special Agent Baker apparently believes in me, too. She and a guy she's dating ate at the *Beach Bar* and the *Cove* a few times when Dawn and I ran into them. She and Dawn have become friends, and she and her boyfriend are here this afternoon.

Like I figured, things have settled down now in VA Beach since Jimmy and his friends are no longer among the living. My abductor who was shot and incinerated in the warehouse fire has been all but forgotten about, so Rikki's crew are in the clear.

Bayside is doing better than ever. Cindy has really blossomed, even more than I thought she would.

Murph has been working hard, getting the boat brokerage up and running. That business seems to suit him well, and he's added a couple of brokers who are making sales. Soon he won't be having to put nearly as much time into it.

Eric, Candi, and Missy came down in his helicopter. Looking at it from here sitting over on the pad, it looks like an adventure machine. I've been looking at helicopter brokerage websites ever since that day I watched the FBI chopper land on the beach. I love flying, and choppers are some of the most complex machines in the air, and a challenge to fly. Maybe one day.

"A Bell 407." Dawn was sliding her arm in mine, having just climbed the stairs to join me.

"What?"

She smiled. "A Bell 407 is what you should get. A good used one costs less to buy than what Eric's Sikorsky does to operate for a year. You only live once, Case. Life is too short for you to stay on the ground. Get the Bell."

I smiled back. Yep, I got it right on the third try.

A FEW AUTHOR NOTES

If you enjoyed Coastal Caper, I'd be grateful if you would leave a review on its page at Amazon.com and on BookBub and GoodReads if you use them. And please email me at contact@ DonRichBooks.com if you would like to let me know what you liked about this book, or the series. I'd love to hear from you! Thanks so much for reading this story, and I hope you'll continue to follow these characters in their future episodes.

Remember, you can sign up for my Reader's Group at www.Don-RichBooks.com and find information about upcoming releases!

Some of your favorite new characters will return in the next installment of the Coastal Adventure Series, Book #7, Coastal Culprit. Murph gets left by himself at *Mallard Cove* while everyone is in Maryland at Casey and Dawn's wedding. What could possibly go wrong? Plenty, of course!

ABOUT THE AUTHOR

Don Rich is the author of the bestselling Coastal Adventure Series. Three of his books even simultaneously held the top three spots in Amazon's Hot New Releases in Boating.

Don's books are set mainly in the mid-Atlantic because of his love for this stretch of coastline. A fifth generation Florida native who grew up on the water, he has spent a good portion of his life on, in, under, or beside it.

He now makes his home in central Virginia. When he's not writing or watching another fantastic mid-Atlantic sunset, he can often be found on the Chesapeake or the Atlantic with a fishing rod in his hand.

Don loves to hear from readers, and you can reach him via email at contact@donrichbooks.com

ALSO BY DON RICH

(Click on titles for more information)

- COASTAL CONSPIRACY
- COASTAL COUSINS
- COASTAL PAYBACKS
- COASTAL TUNA
- COASTAL CATS
- COASTAL CAPER
- COASTAL CULPRIT
- GhostWRITER

Coming later in 2021:

- COASTAL CURSE

Click *HERE* for more information about joining my **Reader's Group**! And you can follow me on Facebook at: https://www. facebook.com/DonRichBooks

I'm also a member of TropicalAuthors.com where you can find my latest books and those of several of my coastal writer friends by clicking on the logo below:

TROPICALAUTHORS.COM

Made in the USA
Middletown, DE
30 July 2021

45071129R00119